Bury Me in Gold Lamé

By Stanton Forbes

BURY ME IN GOLD LAMÉ
SOME POISONED BY THEIR WIVES
WELCOME, MY DEAR, TO BELFRY HOUSE
BUT I WOULDN'T WANT TO DIE THERE
ALL FOR ONE AND ONE FOR DEATH
THE SAD, SUDDEN DEATH OF MY FAIR LADY
IF LAUREL SHOT HARDY THE WORLD WOULD END
SHE WAS ONLY THE SHERIFF'S DAUGHTER
THE NAME'S DEATH, REMEMBER ME?
GO TO THY DEATHBED
IF TWO OF THEM ARE DEAD
ENCOUNTER DARKNESS
A BUSINESS OF BODIES
TERROR TOUCHES ME
RELATIVE TO DEATH
TERRORS OF THE EARTH
GRIEVE FOR THE PAST

Bury Me
in Gold Lamé

STANTON FORBES

PUBLISHED FOR THE CRIME CLUB BY

DOUBLEDAY & COMPANY, INC.

GARDEN CITY, NEW YORK

1974

Library of Congress Cataloging in Publication Data

Forbes, Stanton, 1923–
    Bury me in gold lamé.
    I. Title.
PZ4.F69255Bt [PS3556.067]   813'.5'4
ISBN 0-385-07258-9
Library of Congress Catalogue Number 73–22787

PROLOGUE

To Richard Benson, Attorney at Law,

I, Harrington Hartford Lake, being of reasonably sound mind and body, do hereby take it upon myself to do a rewrite upon my last will and testament and you, Richard, dear boy, will whip it into its proper legal form posthaste, won't you, that's a good lad.

Perhaps it's because of my calendar years and perhaps, too, I'm a bit at loose ends because my bride has gone out shopping for the day, but whatever the cause I feel inclined to summarize, if such a thing is possible, my relationships with my legatees. It seems there are many of these as I look down my list, all of whom I am, mea culpa, responsible for. You'll note, Richard, that I end a sentence with a preposition which brings to mind that fantastic public figure (and not a bad actor when it comes to that) Winston Churchill who spoke eloquently for the despised preposition when he said . . . what was it he said? I do believe my faculty of total recall is weakening, just the other day I could not bring to mind the whole of Hamlet's graveyard speech, alas, poor Yorick, I knew him well.

A fie upon senility! I shall never bow to it, when I have completed this epistle I shall seek out my dog-eared copy of the miseries of the Dane and refresh my memory cells. Where was I? Ah, yes, my heirs. There are times when I say, like Lear, that—how does it go, something, something no sharper tooth than an ungrateful child? Odds, bodkins, I shall have to restudy my Lear as well!

To the point. Let us begin with the one who has been with me the longest, my eldest daughter, indeed my eldest child, Henrietta. A very sensible young woman whom I find excruciatingly dull. But faithful. Oh, yes, ever faithful. Even now as my bride and I continue our honeymoon at the family homestead, Henrietta does all that she can to make us comfortable. She is gracious to my bride, she is solicitous of our well-being, I cannot find a flaw in her attitude and yet, like Regan, Lear's loving child, you see, I do remember that, I would leave her live her own circumspect life and, rather, seek out the companionship of—perhaps my second daughter, Pandora.

Ah, Pandora, willful, vain, ever-demanding, almost unbearable upon occasion. And yet, unlike Henrietta, alive, thrill-seeking, excited and exciting. If only she were more intelligent.

Now, Adam, my youngest son is intelligent. The intellectual of the quintet. His mind is sharp, his words even sharper. I do not care for him, actually, but the fact that I sired him, that I contributed genes to create this highly developed brain, flatters me.

As for the twins, they are now, as they have always been, a bit of an enigma. I can recall when they were small, all arms and legs and huge eyes and mouths full of braces, how like some strange two-headed monster they appeared, staring at me while their mother bade them bid "Daddy good night." Delilah, beautiful creature that she was, should have been a hausfrau. She had all the instincts.

I spoke of Adam and my genes; I must not forget his mother, Aileen, who shares the honors for the creation of this man-child. Aileen is shrewd, but so high-strung. Toward the end of our marriage, I found her quite un-nerving. I believe she sought psychiatric care following our divorce. Yes, I'm sure she did. I remember paying for it.

And last, but not least, there is my young and exquisite bride, *née* Virginia Klineschmidt, that name so amuses me, whom I prefer to call by her exotic stage name, Kohinoor. It fits her, I think. A rare jewel with rough edges. But she will learn. She is young, she is willing, I shall cut her facets with great care until she glitters like the sun.

Forgive me, my friend, if I get carried away. Love is an obsession and thus interesting mainly to the participants. Let us get down to those prickly brass tacks.

When I die, I shall divide my assets thusly:

I

The telephone rang.

Afterward, she was to tell Bruce, "It rang—funny. I just knew something else was about to happen. Honestly. You don't believe me, but it's the truth."

She answered the phone and a nasal, faraway voice asked, "Is this Henrietta Lake?"

"It is."

"This is an overseas call, a Mrs. Pandora Keltie from Paris. Will you accept the charges?"

She's run out of money again, thought Henrietta. "Yes, I'll accept the charges."

She heard clicks and a French conversation that sounded as though it were being held underwater and then came the unmistakable voice of Pandora who might as well have been underwater, too, because every syllable dripped with unshed tears; a very nice performance thought Henrietta without malice.

"Henny, darling! Is it true?"

"Yes, Pandora. Harry died two days ago. A heart attack, very sudden. He didn't suffer."

"I can't believe it. I just can't believe it! He was so eternal, so young for his age, and so careful of his health. Where . . . how did it happen? All your cable said was, 'Father passed away. Funeral Thursday.'"

"They were here at the house; they came back from Miami

Beach last week; Harry hated the place, but she loved it. Anyway, we'd lunched; he was feeling mellow. They went upstairs to nap and he died in his sleep. It was a very nice way to go, Pandora. Please don't get all upset. He was, after all, seventy-one years old. Almost seventy-two."

"Did that woman have anything to do with it? Never mind, I know what you'll say. You're so damned good-hearted, Henny. You'll just have to put off the funeral for another day or so because I want to be there and I can't get on a flight until Thursday."

"But, Pandora, it really isn't necessary. He's been cremated and everything's arranged."

"I don't care!" The drippy tones gave way to Pandora's normal demanding voice. "He's my father, too, and I want to be there. Just because you're the oldest . . ."

Henrietta suppressed a sigh. "You can be here by Friday?"

"Yes, we'll arrive Thursday evening. You'll have to cable me some money."

"We?"

"Jason Jones, a dear friend, has volunteered to come with me. A thousand should do it. I need a bit for my hotel bill and there'll be a few other things to take care of."

"But I just sent you five thousand three weeks ago."

"Henny, darling, Paris is dreadfully expensive, especially now that the dollar counts for less. Be a good girl and cable right away, will you? Pandora's coming home!"

Goody, goody, thought Henrietta, and when she'd hung up she wrote neatly on a pad marked THINGS TO DO TODAY "Cable $1,000 to Pandora, ready two bedrooms, put off funeral." Already written there was "weed garden, take Dorothy to doctor." She wondered if Kohinoor was up yet, such a ridiculous name. Father's fifth wife had been an exotic dancer with the stage name of Kohinoor Diamond before she married Harrington Lake. And Kohinoor preferred, Harry had said, to be called Kohinoor rather than Virginia. Her given name was Virginia Klineschmidt, Henrietta happened to know because she'd seen it on the wedding certificate.

Bruce distracted her, cheeping from his cage, and she stopped to speak to him, telling him she knew the phone call meant trouble. "And just wait until I hear from the rest of them," she concluded.

"Pretty, pretty," said Bruce. It was the only word she'd been able to teach the parakeet.

"Not very pretty, pretty," she said and went upstairs.

Kohinoor was still in bed, of course. It was, after all, only ten in the morning and Kohinoor normally slept till noon or after. Henrietta, having knocked and entered without invitation, stood by the bed and looked down at the titian hair showing on the pillow. Clouds of red silk, her father had called it, describing her new stepmother. "You'll like her, Henny; she's a lovely girl."

"Girl, Harry?"

"Well, she is a bit younger than you, but very mature."

"How young, Harry?"

He'd hemmed and hawed, his distinguished voice making the muttering sound important. "She's—ah—she was thirty-one years old in December." And even though this, too, had been a telephone conversation, she could see him as he said it, handsome silver head inclined at a humble angle, dark eyes begging her approval, mouth set in the famous Lake wry grin in which one corner turned up most appealingly.

"Kohinoor," she spoke softly now and, getting no response, pulled the drapes from the wide window bay, letting in a flood of sunlight. "Kohinoor, I must speak to you. Afterwards, you may go back to sleep."

The head of red hair moved; the sleepy voice made waking sounds, said, "What?" and Henrietta's stepmother rolled over on her back, opened large green eyes, batted very long thick lashes, repeated herself, "What?"

"I've just had a call from Pandora. She's asked that we delay the funeral so that she can attend the services."

"Oh, hell!" said the grieving widow. "Have we got to put it off?"

"I think we must. She is, after all, a daughter."

Kohinoor pushed her pillows high, propped her head up with them, blinked once more, yawned, asked, "What about the rest of them? Any word?"

"Not yet."

"I suppose they'll pick their own days—maybe we should have a whole week of funerals, one for everybody."

"Don and Dawn are in New York, they should have no trouble getting here, nor Aileen, also in the city, nor Adam in Princeton. If they're coming. There's only Delilah from the West Coast . . . well, if you agree, I'll call Mr. Mortimor and tell him Saturday rather than Thursday."

The head turned, buried itself in the pillows. "I suppose so"—in muffled tones—"I just want to get it over with. It's been such a strain on me."

"Of course it has. Shall I pull the curtains shut again?"

"I guess so. At least when I'm asleep, I don't think about Harry." She sounded desolate; poor little girl has lost her doll, thought Henrietta. Drapes drawn, she tiptoed out, went downstairs and telephoned the funeral director.

"Mr. Mortimor, can we put the funeral services off until Saturday? My sister is coming from Paris." She always referred to the others as sisters and brothers, never half-sisters, half-brothers.

"Oh dear." Mr. Mortimor had what Henrietta thought of

as a fruity voice. "I've already notified the papers. I do hope
they haven't gone to press. I'll have to call them this minute."

"You did state that they were private, didn't you? So it
really doesn't matter that much. Same time, same place,
everything the same, Mr. Mortimor, except the day. And
emphasis on the private. All right?"

"Yes, well, I'll do my best with the newspapers. I gave
them the death notice you dictated."

She'd barely hung up when the phone rang again. She
raised her eyebrows at Bruce and answered.

"Henrietta, this is Aileen. I just wanted to tell you I'm
coming to the funeral and so is Adam."

"I wasn't sure——" Henrietta began.

"Of course I am! I was his wife, wasn't I? He is—was the
father of my son. And I'll tell you something else, Henny,
I think it's very strange—he married some young woman,
some strange young woman, and two months later, he's
dead."

"They were here in this house when it happened, Aileen.
Kohinoor is, at this moment, prostrate in bed. And Dr. Hen-
derson said it was a heart attack, signed the death certificate.
So please don't come here intending to start trouble."

"Me? Start trouble?" Aileen's fashionable eyebrows were
V-shaped. Henrietta could visualize the height of them
now, the disdainful look down the classic nose. "I'm not a
troublemaker, Henrietta, you know that. We got along very
well when I was married to your father. It's just that I must
protect Adam. Heaven knows what that woman got Harrington to do with his will."

Of course, thought Henrietta, that's it. And ten to one
that's why Pandora's coming, too. She should have suspected
it immediately. She supposed they'd all come, the gathering of the clan Lake, even Delilah. The crows picking at the

carrion. She told Aileen the new date of the funeral, added, "I'll have two rooms ready for you here. I presume you plan to stay overnight at the house."

"If it's not inconvenient." Aileen could purr.

"No, Pandora's coming, too. From Paris on Friday morning."

"We'll arrive the same day by car. Adam's coming here from Princeton. I told him this morning how fortunate it was that you were in charge. Dear Henrietta, so faithful, so reliable."

Enough of that, thought Henrietta. They'd put that on her tombstone, no doubt, Henrietta, so faithful, so reliable, lies here. "I'll see you Friday then."

"I'm sending flowers."

"I'm not sure that's necessary. It's a memorial service; he's been cremated."

"Cremated?" Aileen sounded as though she'd swallowed little bits of glass. "If I were you I'd have had an autopsy first. Did you have an autopsy?"

Wearily, "No, Aileen. Dr. Henderson was very sure. And there isn't anything we can do about it now; it's been done."

"Well, I think you've made a mistake. Personally, I'd want to be very certain——"

"I am, Aileen. Very certain. I'll expect you and Adam on Friday." And she hung up the phone, exasperated. Aileen had been her favorite stepmother but, unlike wine, had not improved with age.

She checked her watch; time, she thought, to weed some before lunch, being in the garden always soothed her. She'd go through the kitchen and tell Ingrid that there'd be guests —for the weekend? Who knew? That depended, she supposed, on Richard Benson and the reading of the will.

Ingrid was busy at the stove, took the news with her usual

sour expression and the comment, "I'll need some extra help with four new people. Better get my cousin Hilda, yes?"

Cousin Hilda, Henrietta recalled, was even larger than the solid Ingrid who might have qualified for a pro linebacker had she been male. "Yes, get Hilda. I don't know for how long, the weekend at least. Will Thor be all right?" Thor was Ingrid's husband and, despite his name, a little man. Or maybe he only looked small next to Ingrid.

"We'll see. If not, I get my cousin Karl."

"Do what you think best." Ingrid could recruit a small army of cousins if need be. "I'm going out to the garden. I'll come in at noon."

From the potting shed, Henrietta took hat, gloves, kneeling pad, and trowel. The lilies of the valley along the path were all abloom; lovely little wild flowers, they looked as though they should tinkle when a breeze blew through.

The natural garden was aflower as well, daphne among the rocks, iris, star-of-Bethlehem, and bleeding heart.

And the flowering shrubs, azaleas and rhododendron, mountain laurels. Bulbs—hyacinth, narcissus and daffodil— even rhubarb, coming along nicely at the back of the vegetable plot. Hector, the sheep dog, found her then, lumbered up for a pat; he wasn't allowed in the house and so always seemed lonely. He followed her along the path until he saw a squirrel and took off. Hector, the hunter. Alas, so clumsy.

It was the vegetable garden that needed immediate attention. All the little seedlings had reared tiny green heads, and needed thinning and protection from the pesky weeds. Henrietta lost herself for over an hour and, returning to the house just after twelve, felt rejuvenated. A garden in the spring, heaven on earth, she thought.

Kohinoor was not down yet, Ingrid told her.

"We'll just let her sleep," Henrietta decided. "Save some

soup; she can have that later with a sandwich if she wishes. Have you seen Dorothy? She's to go to the doctor's at one."

Ingrid shook her braided head—she wore her braids over each ear unlike Henrietta's crown—left Henrietta's lunch (steaming vegetable soup, homemade, a salad of pineapple and cottage cheese, iced tea), and retreated to the kitchen. Dorothy was a very intelligent kitten, Henrietta reflected. She probably knew she was going to the vet's to be spayed. A bowl of catnip from the garden should fetch her out. She'd have to stay overnight at the vet's . . . the telephone rang.

Someone answered it because it only rang once. Henrietta put down her soup spoon, waiting. The intercom buzzed and she answered. Kohinoor said, "Henrietta, it's for you." Henrietta was warned by the tone of her voice. She went to the phone and spoke into it.

"This is Delilah, Henny. What happened to Harrington? I see that woman is there. The funeral's Thursday? We're coming. Don and Dawn will drive from New York and I will fly out. I'm between pictures, so we'll stay as long as we're needed."

Henrietta felt like a relay runner, waiting for the perfect timing to grab the conversational baton. "The funeral's been changed to Saturday, Delilah." She wondered if Kohinoor were listening; she couldn't recall hearing the click of the connection.

"Saturday? I'll come on Friday then. When is the will being read? You still haven't told me—how did he die? It must have been sudden. Are you sure there wasn't anything funny about it?"

"He had a heart attack. Yes, it was sudden. There was no pain; he died in his sleep. What time will you be coming Friday?"

"I have a schedule right here. There's a flight arriving in

Hartford at 5:45. I'll be on that. Send the car for me and order some flowers, white roses in my name, something appropriate for Don and Dawn. This call is costing money. I'll see you Friday, Henrietta. Good-by."

Returning to her now cool soup, Henrietta mentally counted bedrooms. They would all be there—Harrington Lake's children—Henrietta, Pandora, Don and Dawn, the twins, and Adam, the youngest. Plus Harrington Lake's surviving wives, Delilah, mother of Don and Dawn; Aileen, mother of Adam; and, of course, Kohinoor, mother of no one. Six more bedrooms, no, seven. Someone named—Jones, was it—was coming with Pandora. A houseful of mourners arriving on Friday. It promised to be some kind of weekend.

Later riding with Dorothy in her lap, in the back seat of the limousine, with Thor driving and the glass partition between closed so that he couldn't hear, she told the cat, "They never got along, never, and I don't suppose they will now."

Dorothy stared up at her with wise yellow eyes and blinked, slowly. Henrietta rubbed Dorothy under the chin and the golden eyes closed.

II

"Jason, darling, be a dear and close that case for me, will you? I seem to have stuffed it too full, but the others are all shut and locked. Thank you, darling. I'll be ready in a minute." Pandora Lake Keltie relaxed her mouth so that she could paint it with her lipstick brush, very carefully, fill in those thin places, ah so, voilà.

She knew she looked younger than her thirty-seven years. She could pass for thirty, she thought, and it was how you looked that was important, not how many mornings you'd gotten up to face a new day.

"Come on, kid." (She liked Jason to call her kid.) "Get with it or you'll make us miss the plane."

"I'm almost ready. Did you call the desk for a porter?"

"I can carry these three big bags if you'll take the small one and the jewel case."

Pandora wrinkled her nose at him in the mirror. "Darling, that would be gauche. Do call the desk. And get my mink out of the closet." The porter came quickly; he damn well should, the money she'd shelled out for this suite in recent weeks . . . and M. Bodin at the desk had expressed "devastation" at losing "the beautiful Madame Keltie" and kissed her hand. As it should be—a triumphant exit—Pandora looking elegant in mink and diamonds, Jason looking handsome and somehow feral in the new camel's-hair coat she'd bought him. "*Bon jour, bon jour, merci!*" And out to the taxi, a large tip for the porter, something for the doorman who handed her into the cab.

"Ah," she said, settling back and looking at her diamond wristwatch, "we have plenty of time."

Jason took a gold cigarette case from his inside pocket, removed a cigarette, and lit it with matching lighter. She'd given those to him on their three-month anniversary. He drew deeply on the cigarette, exhaled smoke, and said, "What did your sister say when you told her I was coming?"

"Henrietta? She's my half-sister—same father, different mothers. She didn't say anything. Why should she?"

Jason shrugged, narrowed his eyes until Pandora thought he looked like a pirate, decided he needed his sunshades. With them on he looked like an apache dancer. He had the same facility as her father—the ability to appear to be several different men with no effort, or no seeming effort. Was he aware of his guises? Probably.

She had champagne at the airport; Jason drank martinis. They flew first class, of course, and after more champagne and martinis, Pandora dozed while Jason slept.

She dreamed pictures of her father, old still photos; Harrington Lake and her mother at the shore on a warm August day; her father sunning on a beach blanket, his lean figure turning mahogany as they watched, or so it seemed. He must have been fortyish then. Pandora was five years old that summer. And Mother, Audrey Dell to the rest of the world, swimming furiously, trying, as always, to work some of the chubbiness off. Weight had always been a problem with Audrey; finally killed her in a way, didn't it? Yes, didn't it.

Henny had been there that day, naturally. Where else? She would have been sixteen or seventeen years of age then, but she'd not gone away to school nor to summer camp nor to visit friends; she'd never really left home. Not Henny. "Henny's my home girl," Father had often said.

Anyway, Henny had been there, lying a little way off and reading a book. Pandora could see her, the no-color hair, well, blond but not quite, caught back in pigtails, short skimpy pigtails, looking all wrong, glancing up from her book, saying, "Harry, that child is getting all sunburned." Henny was the only one who called their father Harry to his face; that was odd; she made it sound as though she was his equal.

Father had lifted his head up, he was lying on his stomach, and crinkled his eyes at Pandora. "Oh, pussycat, little pink one, do cover up or something."

"Yes, Daddy." She didn't move. She never had to do what he said; he said it and forgot it.

Henny went back to reading her book. Pandora deliberately gave herself to the sun. Go ahead, I dare you, burn me, burn me.

Father turned over on his back, covered his eyes with his arm. The sea swished.

"Harry, it's just possible that your wife might drown."

Father opened his eyes, blinked at Henrietta, looked seaward. "Audrey," he called, "shouldn't you come in now?" He returned to his previous position, eyes again hidden, and Pandora thought, She's too far out, she can't hear him.

Watching Henny, Henny was the one to watch, Pandora saw Henny look for a few minutes, return to her book. She could almost see the title of Henrietta's book after all these years—what was it? She couldn't read then. That's why she couldn't remember.

Pandora's skin began to feel hot. She touched a shoulder with tentative fingers. When she pressed down the skin was yellow; the rest was pink, very pink. She was getting sunburned—now she'd know what it felt like. She reached for a towel, edged toward the beach umbrella set up on the sand. Just like that icky Henny to be right. She'd never give Henny the satisfaction of complaining. The sun was very hot, even under the umbrella. Some kind of bee or wasp, something, buzzed around her sweaty face.

A gull squealed.

No, not a gull.

Mother. Mother, way out in the sea, made a sound like a gull. A trouble sound.

Pandora sat bolt upright.

Henny dropped her book.

"Harry," she said, "Audrey needs help."

"What? What?" Father struggled to sit up.

Pandora screamed, "Mother!" and ran toward the sea.

Mother was waving her arms and bobbing up and down far out in the brilliant blue water. "Help," shrilled Pandora. "Help my mother!"

She looked back, Father was just getting off his blanket; Henny was running across the sand, thin arms and legs pumping up and down.

Father came roaring past them, an express train, and threw himself into the water. Pandora, heart pounding so that she thought it would break, stopped, hip-high in the ocean, Henny just ahead. They watched together.

And when Father came in, towing Mother, fighting the tide, they helped him haul her onto the sand and watched again while he began, frantically, to give artificial respiration. Pandora heard Henny say in a faraway voice, "At last she got his attention."

"What's the matter with you?" asked Jason.

"What?" She was startled. "Nothing. Nothing's the matter with me."

"You were making little noises in your sleep."

"I was? I didn't think I was sleeping." She reached out, demanded, "Give me a cigarette."

He obliged. "What were you dreaming about?"

"Was I dreaming? I don't remember. Ring for the steward. I'd like some more champagne." And the second glass put her back to sleep, and she didn't dream again all the way to New York.

Customs was, as usual, a bore. As was the ride to Connecticut in the taxi they hired. The cabbie thought himself a conversationalist until Pandora told him to kindly drive and be silent; she wanted to sleep. She was still sleeping when Jason shook her gently and told her, "I think we're here."

Pandora sat up, yawned, and smoothed her hair under her Pucci turban. "A very impressive house," said Jason.

"Yes, I suppose so. It's old, of course. How much do we owe you, driver?" He gave her a surly answer which she ignored, counted bills, added a tip, and climbed out of the cab with Jason's help. The cabbie, silent still but now looking agreeable—the tip had been a generous one but so what, money was only money—carried the bags up the wide steps between the pillars. The door opened as they followed him, and Henrietta welcomed Pandora home.

Good heavens, thought Pandora, she's gone completely gray. "Darling, Henny! You look wonderful." She bent and kissed the smooth cheek, still thinking, but not a wrinkle; how does she do it? She must be nearly fifty. "This is Jason Jones. My sister, Henrietta Lake."

"Thank you for allowing me to come," said Jason, bending over Henrietta's hand. One of Jason's many attractive qualities was his excellent manners, when he wished to use them. Pandora couldn't abide a gauche male.

A small blond man, clad in butler's uniform, was introduced as Thor; he brought the luggage in. "Heavens, Pan-

dora"—Henny looked amused—"do you always travel so
lightly?" She was being sarcastic, of course; she'd always had
that wry and, to Pandora, slightly unpleasant sense of humor.

"Only four of the cases are mine," she answered airily. "The
small one belongs to Jason. Actually, there's more coming.
I had to ship it all. I don't know how long we'll be here or
where we'll be going next."

"This is an elegant house, Miss Lake." Jason was looking
around the octangular reception hall.

"It was built just after the turn of the century by a stockbroker who, fortunately, hired an architect with taste. That
saved it from being the usual monstrosity of the era. The
stockbroker lost his money and Harry, Father, bought it, a
great bargain. I've lived here all my life"—a smile, that
dimple she'd inherited from her mother, flashed—"and that's
a long time."

Jason had a way of smiling depreciatively. Thank God he
never paid the obvious compliment. Another man, interested
in making an impression, might have answered, "Not so long,"
or "Maybe X-number of years ago," making sure the X number was low, but not Jason. He just smiled that smile which
said, Come now, you're still young. Henny got the message,
too, Pandora could tell. Don't get any ideas, Henny, she told
her silently. He's mine and you are too old. I'm not, but you
are!

III

Don was driving and Don was drunk. Not falling down drunk, nothing like that; in fact most people wouldn't realize he was blotto, but Dawn knew, as she always knew, what her brother was feeling, thinking.

Because he was drunk, he was driving slowly, and cars coming up behind him on the Merritt Parkway were passing, their drivers glaring as they passed, because he was driving so slowly. Dawn didn't complain nor offer to drive, she knew better. Don had to do what Don wished to do. Well, so did she and he respected that, too. He was the only person she knew who did.

"She killed him," he said, breaking the fifteen-minute-or-so silence. "I knew it would happen one day. She killed him."

"Mother said that Henny said it was a heart attack."

"Everybody dies from a heart attack. That's what happens when you die; your heart stops beating and that's a heart attack."

She glanced at him, knew his eyes behind the lavender-tinted sunglasses were slightly out of focus. "Are you going to accuse her? You can't unless you know how she did it."

He laughed. His longish fair hair, thinning just a little, poor Don, stirred in the small breeze. "I know how she killed him." And he leered at the road ahead.

"Oh, that. I suppose if you're old enough, too old, over-exertion would do it. Still, who said, what a way to go?"

He turned his grin on her, loosened his mouth to laugh again. She laughed back, changed the subject. "Where were you yesterday? And the day before? You didn't say you were going anywhere."

"Tomcatting." He turned his face back toward the road. She thought her brother was very handsome. That was a form of self-love, wasn't it? Because they looked much the same?

"Anyone I know?"

"Nope. You wouldn't care for Phyllis."

"If you say so." Her own hair, lighter than his, but then she had to use a bleach—if you were going to be a blonde in the entertainment business, you had to be a pale blonde for the camera—blew away from her neck. She stroked it gently; she loved to feel her own hair, so long, so soft. She washed it every day, never went to a hairdresser except for color, let it dry naturally, and it obligingly went its own beautiful way, waving just enough where it should, hanging straight where it should. Good hair, better than Don's actually. She'd gotten the best of the hair deal, if nothing else. One twin always got the best from the other; why was it never even Stephen?

"We've got to be back by Monday," Don said suddenly. "I hope they get the will business over quick."

"Why Monday?"

"I've got a new taping. Didn't Arlen tell you?"

"Just because we have the same agent doesn't mean I know what you know. What's the product?"

He wrinkled his aristocratic nose. "Some new deodorant. I'm supposed to loll in bed, looking sexy and handsome and all that stuff, and sell the junk."

She thought back. "At least it's better than the deodorant commercial I did a couple of years ago. Remember, the one when everybody ran away from me and I couldn't figure out what was wrong?"

Don laughed. "That was a bummer. I'm thirsty. Let's stop in New Haven and get a drink."

"It's just a little farther to the house. Why not get a drink there? For free?"

"And have Henny, dear Henny, laughing behind that tolerant face?"

"So let her laugh."

"The trouble with Henny is that she's never had a man." A car behind them honked impatiently and Don muttered, shifted to low, slowed the MG down even more.

Dawn, watching the middle-aged man in the car behind, giggled. "He'd like to run right over us if he could." The lane to the left finally free, the Cadillac—huge ugly thing, thought Dawn—roared past them. "How do you know Henny's never had a man?"

"I can smell a dyed-in-the-wool virgin."

"I'll bet you can." She leaned back and they fell into one of their comfortable silences. He was the only man she'd ever felt she could be silent with. But that was because they were twins. She'd read studies about twins—it seemed there was something to that invisible-bond business, an unseen umbilical cord. "I wonder," she mused aloud, "how much he'll leave us."

"Plenty, let's hope. I could use plenty."

"Ummm. He had plenty." She clapped her hands like a child. "Plenty for all. Mother's expecting a bundle, too."

"Maybe not. There's been two wives since. He might have figured he's paid her enough."

"She doesn't think so. And they parted amicably."

"She thinks they parted amicably."

"Well, didn't they?"

"How should I know? I was four."

"So was I."

"Yes, you were, weren't you? God, I'm parched."

"Drive faster, then. We'll get there quicker."

"Good thinking." And he pushed the accelerator to the floor, making the engine roar and sending the car surging forward like a horse from a starting gate. He entered the passing lane with a swoosh and her hair flew free—an ornament, she was, on an old radiator cap. They caught up with the Cadillac after a little way and zoomed past, honking the MG's horn and laughing at the expression on the middle-aged face of its driver.

Speeding into the long drive that led to the house a bit later, they nearly rammed a limousine unexpectedly there, and the startled face that looked at them from the back seat was the imperious visage of their mother, known to three generations of movie audiences as Delilah Heap.

Don sounded the horn, kept sounding it as they swerved off the drive to pass the limousine, and kept the sound going all the way up to the house. He braked the car with a squeal of tires and turned off the engine. Then he fell back against the seat and slid down in it, his legs stretched out, eyes closed, mouth slightly open. We just made it, thought Dawn. That's very exciting.

IV

She looks even thinner than usual, thought Adam Lake, watching his mother maneuver her Thunderbird. But God, she's got style.

"Light me a cigarette, Adam, please. Thank heavens we're almost there. Driving exhausts me. My cigarettes and lighter are right on top in my pocketbook."

Adam found them, did as he was told, handed the lit cigarette over. "Ever considered giving these up?"

Aileen Patton Lake reached eagerly for the cigarette. "I couldn't possibly. I'd blow up like a balloon. And a girl can't run a modeling agency, my pet, with a figure like Totie Fields'." She took a long puff, inhaled deeply, asked idly, "Any problems at school? You haven't called me lately."

"Sorry, Mother. I haven't written either, I know. Diplomacy is not an easy field, yet diplomacy should begin, like charity, at home."

She stole a glance at him. "How impressive. Does that mean you've been spending your nights gambling again?"

"Playing bridge is not gambling."

"Ho, ho." Her profile was marvelous, Adam thought. All that chiseled bone. He resembled his father, not his mother, but that wasn't bad either.

"When I run short on cash, I don't like to bug you about it. I know you run short yourself, sometimes. So I find a friendly game. It doesn't hurt anyone."

"If you win."

"Don't I always?"

"Not always."

"Yes, well, sorry about that one time. I had a streak of bad luck."

"A ten-thousand-dollar streak." She sounded more sad than bitter.

"I'm sorry; you know I am. I know how tough it was for you to come up with it. If that Spencer had just carried me a little longer, but he's a freak."

"I don't understand. What do you spend it all on? I mean, your tuition, your dorm, all those things are paid . . ."

"Little things, Mom, little things. It's hard to explain."

"In other words, don't pry?"

"I didn't say that. You know we have an honest relationship. Free and open."

She didn't answer and, in his opinion, that was just as well. You couldn't tell your mother everything.

After a moment though she said, "A girl?"

"No, Mom. No girl. No special one, that is." He took another tack. "When do you think they'll read the will?"

She looked up at him, aghast? Put on? Real? "Don't you care that your father is dead?"

In this, he could level with her. "Not very much. He just never seemed real to me. You know, you go to the films or the theater and you watch this larger-than-life character, and then somebody says, that's your father."

"Yes, I understand. But he wasn't like that at home."

"The hell he wasn't!"

"You mustn't think he didn't love you."

"Mustn't I?" He laughed. "You're getting emotional, Mom. I know he loved me, of course I do! He loved all his children—Henrietta, Pandora, Don and Dawn, good old Don and Dawn, and little ole me." He patted her shoulder. "Look, I'm just putting you on. You picked a fabulous father for yours truly."

She sighed. "You don't know what he was like, really. On an adult basis. I was a young—and so green—model. From Indianapolis. Suddenly in New York. Suddenly much in demand. Wide-eyed, but wise. I mean, no stupid young man, no matter how pretty. And then—Harrington Lake, good heavens, can you imagine what a god he was? As a girl, a young girl, I would go to the movies and there was that face. When I got to New York, I saw my first live theater. And who did I see? Harrington Lake as Hamlet. I was overwhelmed when I met him, when he asked me out. And then, when he asked me to marry him . . ." She gave Adam a wry smile. "I'm sorry. I'm embarrassing you."

"Me? Not me. What kind of a husband was he, anyway? I never found out. I was always away at school."

She said, proudly, he thought, "I stayed married to him the longest. Seventeen years. And he waited the longest to remarry after me—six years later." She stubbed out the cigarette butt in the car ashtray. "I wonder what she's like, the new one?"

"You're changing the subject."

"How was he to live with? Never dull, my dear. Never dull."

"You aren't going to tell me."

"It's too long a story. And all over with. Definitely. All over with."

"Why did he marry you?"

Her mouth tightened; she was getting irritated. "You may not believe it, but I was a very beautiful young woman in my day. Even though you may not believe it."

He placated her. "Oh, come on. Of course I believe it. You're still beautiful. Why did he leave you?"

"He didn't. You were there, you should know."

"I wasn't there. As I said, I was always away at school. Did he always marry beautiful women?"

"Always. He couldn't help the way he was. He'd meet a new one and that new one would become the one. He couldn't help it."

"Did he have to marry them all?"

"He wouldn't have considered it any other way. He was an honorable man. And even though he had five wives, he lost two of them in tragic ways. Henrietta's mother took her own life and Pandora's mother drowned. Who knows, if either of them had lived, things might have been different."

"And then there would have been no me."

She stole another glance; his tone hadn't matched his words. "Something is bothering you."

Adam laughed. "Nothing is bothering me. I inherited my Hamlet tendencies from dear old Dad. Come on, girl, step on the gas, push the accelerator down to the floor. I'm anxious for a grand-and-glorious, wide-screen, technicolor family reunion."

V

The urn, standing on the mantel in the big living room, seemed to be two urns, reflected as it was in the huge, gold-framed mirror.

Jason Jones was tending bar. Pandora, sipping Pernod, could see him in the mirror mixing things, saying something to Dawn who looked, Pandora thought, like hell warmed over. Those wide-legged pants, like something out of the thirties. Thirties styles were supposed to be very chic, Pandora knew, but it took a certain flair to wear them well, and poor Dawn simply didn't have it. All that stringy blond hair hanging down her back and no make-up. She was supposed to be a very successful TV actress, soap operas and commercials mainly. Pandora couldn't imagine why; she looked so—ordinary.

"I keep looking at that urn and thinking, Harrington Lake can't be in there. He just can't!" Delilah, ex-stepmother, good old bitchy Delilah, was the speaker, standing behind Pandora, clutching an ember-colored concoction in a long-nailed hand. Not a platinum hair out of place, Delilah was holding up well. How old was she now? In her fifties at least. It must take a lot of time and effort to maintain that slim figure, that supple-seeming skin.

Pandora, who had been avoiding the urn, shrugged. "It's as good a resting place as any, I suppose."

"I thought he'd be buried in the vault with Clara and

Audrey. I can't imagine why he'd want to be cremated." She shivered. "All that fire. It's barbaric."

Adam joined them; his drink looked to be a martini. "I'd guess he chose cremation so he could continue to be the center of attention." A handsome young man was Adam; how much he looked like Father at first glance, thought Pandora. But only at first glance. Father had exuded an aura of confidence, success. There was a look in Adam's eyes that made Pandora think of a man peering out through prison bars.

"Don't be snide, Adam." This from Aileen, carrying a paler tan drink. Scotch, no doubt. Nobody drank the same thing? Jason was getting a workout. Watching him in the mirror, Pandora saw him take a drink to the grieving widow who sat all alone on one of the long sofas flanking the fireplace. She reminded Pandora of a big, red-haired, healthy-looking animal. Good God, was she for real? Pandora estimated the measurements, properly encased in black silk, as 40-28-36.

Don Lake plopped down on the sofa near her. "Want my handkerchief?" he offered. He and Dawn were twins, true, but the look looked better on him. Rather satanic, Pandora decided. A blond devil. He'd been soused when he arrived and stayed, more or less, that way. But he handled it well. Pandora knew because it took a drinker to know a drinker. And she considered herself an expert.

Kohinoor shook that mass of red hair sadly at Don, produced her own bit of cloth, white, lace-edged of course, what else? She touched her eyes with it. Perpetually tear-filled, those green eyes, really green, again Pandora thought of an animal. What kind? A cat? No, more like some strange kind of green-eyed cow. But cows were placid. Kohinoor didn't look placid.

"Where is Henrietta?" asked the grieving widow.

"Out in the garden, I believe." Jason, bearing his favorite Campari, came and sat on the other side of Kohinoor. "She said something about the comfort of digging in dirt."

"Does anyone know when Richard Benson is coming?" Dawn chose a seat on the opposite sofa. "We hoped to go back on Monday."

Delilah had the answer, naturally. "Not until Monday afternoon. Henrietta said he had a weekend trip planned, so she told him Monday would do. I'm afraid you'll have to stay over."

Dawn made a face, looked at her brother. "I've already called Arlen," he told her, "and put it off until Tuesday."

"Isn't that fine?" asked Adam. "We've got today and Sunday to stand around staring at Harrington Lake in his new role."

Kohinoor burst into tears. Jason patted her shoulder. Pandora made mental notes for a future speech, scheduled for delivery the next time she got Jason alone. "Don't try to weasel in there, darling. Or mama will spank. You're my property, remember?"

But she felt almost like crying, too. Spending an entire weekend in this house with these people—she'd gone away to be free of them. Still, it had to be done. Richard Benson had the will and the will must be read . . . and heard.

She was pretty sure of its provisions. Trust funds for all of them. The question was, How much? And was it an irrevocable trust? Benson could tell her, she'd talk to him and then, voilà, back to Paris or maybe Rome or Madrid, wherever her fancy led her.

"How about a game of bridge?" Adam suggested. "Two tables if Henrietta will play. Maybe a cent a point?"

Kohinoor sniffed, daubed her nose with the handkerchief.

"Someone would have to teach me how. I've never played."

"It's not that hard," Jason assured her. "I'll show you how." I'll bet you would, thought Pandora.

She said, "I'm not in the mood for bridge. Jason, why don't we take a run into town? There used to be a cosy bar at the inn." And she gave him a look that told him he'd better say Yes.

"One table then." Adam rang the servant's bell. "Mother, you and I will take on all comers. What do you say?"

Henrietta appeared in the archway, carrying an armload of flowers. "I'll be with you as soon as I put these in vases. Everyone have everything?"

A petite woman, fair hair turning gray, braided and wound around her head—that's the way one of the lengthy newspaper articles had described Henrietta. The same writer had said that Pandora Lake Keltie was a fashionable woman of indeterminate years with a handsome but discontented face. Really! He'd been much kinder to Henrietta, and even though Pandora knew Henny was said to look like her mother, she'd seen pictures of Clara Patrick in her silent screen heyday and couldn't see the resemblance. Where Clara Patrick had looked ever so young, with sparkling eyes and a cupid's bow mouth, Henny's eyes had always been pale, not lifeless, exactly, but without any kind of passion. And her expression was serene, matronly, her mouth just an ordinary mouth, turning down at the corners just the least bit. Only when she smiled and the dimple appeared did she look anything like Clara Patrick. And she didn't smile often.

"Could Jason and I use a car?" asked Pandora. "We'd like to go into the village."

"Of course, Pandora. Here's Thor now. He'll get you the keys." She looked across the room to the urn, added, "I think these lilies of the valley will look very nice on either side, don't you?" And without waiting for an answer, she went away, taking Thor with her, presumably for keys.

It was Adam who broke the silence by asking, "Was she—am I wrong—was she talking to the urn?"

"Of course not." Aileen spoke at the same time as Dawn who asked, "What if she was?"

Kohinoor pushed herself up from the sofa; Pandora noted that Jason and Don got to their feet immediately. "I'm going up and lie down. I just can't sit here and——" She glanced at the mantel, then away. "I just hate that thing sitting there. It's as though Harrington were——" She had to use the handkerchief. "All I can say is that when I die, I don't want to be put in any old jar! When I die, they can bury me in gold lamé!" And she ran out of the room, sobbing, nearly colliding with Thor who'd appeared again in the archway.

"Anything your little heart desires," Adam called after her. What a brash young man! Pandora found him amusing.

"Adam!" exclaimed his mother.

"Just joshing, Mother dear." He grinned at her. "Now, how about that bridge game?"

VI

Kohinoor locked her bedroom door and threw herself across the bed. They all hated her, she knew that, and as soon as she could she would get out of this house, away. Because she didn't like them either. The only one who was even half-way nice to her was Henrietta and that meant only that Henrietta was polite.

She rolled over. She'd put a girdle on and it was cutting into her in about eight places. She sat up, unfastened her stockings, and wriggled out of it. Reaching back to undo her zipper, damn, it took arms eight feet long. Harrington used to do that for her; he loved doing it, he said, damn . . .

Out the window she could see a part of the gardens and the path to the garage. The ritzy one who came from Paris, Pandora, that was her name, came out with that handsome midnight cowboy, Jason Jones, trailing after. If Kohinoor gave him a look, he'd take the bait, she knew that. But Jason Jones and his kind weren't on her dance list. She didn't want someone to take care of; she wanted someone to take care of her. "Oh, Harrington," she whispered. She missed him—she really did—something awful. He'd been perfect; everything she'd ever wanted in a man. Oh, why did he have to die on her?

She finally managed the back zipper, shucked off the dress, hateful black thing, and let it fall to the floor. From the closet she took a red jersey robe; she always wore red when she could in private because it wasn't supposed to be a red-head's color but she loved it. She unfastened her bra and dropped that, too; God, it felt wonderful to be free.

Free? Who was free? Not Kohinoor Diamond, no, trapped again. Trapped in an old snare, she'd have to go back to work when this was all over.

Well, she didn't hate working. Not all of it. She enjoyed dancing; she even enjoyed dancing before an audience of hard-breathing, perspiring males because they couldn't touch her. They could think what they wanted but they couldn't touch her. The smile she wore when performing, it had been compared to the smile of Mona Lisa, was due to the fact that she knew and they didn't know, couldn't possibly guess, that Kohinoor Diamond was a virgin—still was. That was one of the wonderful things about Harrington Lake.

He'd loved her for herself alone.

Tears came. Why did he have to die so soon? Because of his age? She knew when they married they might have only ten or, at the most, fifteen years together. But only a few weeks? It wasn't fair; it just wasn't fair. He'd been in good health, he'd told her that. "My doctor says I have the physical condition of a much younger man." Nothing at all about a bad heart.

He'd become ill in the afternoon. She was washing her hair, he was lying down, his usual after-lunch custom. She'd come out of the shower, towel around her head, glanced at the bed; Harrington appeared to be sleeping.

She went out on the bedroom balcony, there to brush her hair and dry it in the sun. It was a beautiful day, the grass was a brilliant spring green, the spring garden flowers a mass of color, the sky a vivid, cloudless blue.

Kohinoor, sitting on the chaise longue, brushed enthusi-astically for several minutes, then leaned back and let the warmth of the sun lull her into drowsiness. There was a fly and a spider and a bumblebee and a dragonfly . . . she could hear each of them making tiny noises, it seemed, and smelling the flowers from the garden . . . she had never felt so happy, so safe . . . and after a while, a safe while, when she was even more sure than now, because you could never take anything for granted—things could change overnight, God, she knew that—she'd tell Harrington about Annie and maybe they could bring her to stay with them.

From far away she thought she heard a sound. She opened her eyes, glanced into the bedroom, couldn't see too clearly; there was a sheer curtain over the French doors that opened onto the balcony. He looked to be sleeping peacefully, still she said softly, "Harrington?" He didn't answer and she leaned back in the chaise again, closed her eyes.

Unexpectedly, she fell asleep. What awoke her was a voice; she very clearly heard a voice crying, "Help." Uncertain—had she been dreaming?—she sat upright. The sun had gone from its high point in the sky and the bedroom interior was in shadow. Kohinoor got up, went inside. Harrington's eyes were open, he was looking at her, and she asked, "Is anything wrong? Are you all right?"

He didn't answer, just kept staring. She bent over him, "Harrington, Harry, speak to me." She touched him, then backed away with a little cry. Hands trembling, she spoke into the intercom, "Henrietta, somebody, come! Harrington is—sick."

"I'm coming," Henrietta's calm voice assured her.

Kohinoor went back to the bedside, clasped her hands, pulled at each hand with the other, demanded tearfully, "Harrington, wake up. Tell me what's wrong. Harrington!"

The bedroom door opened quietly, quickly, Henrietta

moved like that, and she came immediately to the other side of the bed, bent over Harrington.

"What is it?" Kohinoor found herself whispering, her voice had vanished.

Henrietta just glanced at her, turned to the phone on the bedside table. She dialed a number and as Kohinoor was asking, "Who are you calling?" she spoke into the mouthpiece. "Dr. Henderson? Henrietta Lake. Could you come out to the house immediately, please? I think something has happened to my father."

And as she hung up, Kohinoor was whispering, kept whispering, kept thinking, oh, no, no, no, no! It's too soon!

Henrietta was very sympathetic, she had to give her credit for that. "Are you all right?" she asked, putting her arms around Kohinoor. And that's when Kohinoor began sobbing and didn't stop until Dr. Henderson came.

He wasn't a young man, but not as old as Harrington. He was a quiet-spoken man. When he came in he said to Henrietta, "Is she all right?" meaning Kohinoor and when Henrietta answered with a gesture that seemed to mean I don't know, Kohinoor cried, "Don't, don't—help him!"

Dr. Henderson, he was a courtly, comforting-looking doctor, bent over the bed as though he'd known from the beginning. He said, raising up from bending over. "I'm afraid he's had a coronary. I'm afraid it's too late."

"No!" Kohinoor told him. "There must be something you can do. Doctors can massage the heart now—do something!"

"I'm sorry," he said and Henrietta, talking to him, said, "He would have wanted it that way. Suddenly."

"Damn you," Kohinoor had cried. "Damn you both!"

"Kohinoor"—Henrietta always said her stage name as though it tasted bad, at least that's the way it sounded to

Kohinoor—"please, my dear. Come with me. He lived a good, long life. You've got to remember that."

"He hadn't finished," she screamed. "Don't you understand that? He hadn't finished! It isn't fair—I need him!" And she burst into tears once more.

"A sedative," murmured Dr. Henderson.

"I'll take her into my room." Henrietta nudged her toward the door.

But Kohinoor broke loose and threw herself across the bed, sobbing, and even as she sobbed, a part of her wondered, Do they think I'm putting this on?

Now, five days later in the same awful room—Henrietta said she couldn't move her to another room because all the others were coming—Kohinoor supposed Henrietta did believe she was pretending grief.

Well, she might not be the brightest person in the world, but Kohinoor wasn't born yesterday either and one thing she did know—they all hated her.

Okay. They wouldn't have to put up with her much longer. As soon as possible, as soon as the will was read, she'd be long gone. In a cloud of dust.

She'd take what he left her—he left her something because he'd said as much—and run for daylight. God knew she'd need the money; it cost so much to keep Annie in that place. Well, as it turned out, it was a good thing she hadn't brought her here for this short time. All that moving back and forth, that would be bad for her, that was for sure.

Oh, Annie, she thought, tears returning, it's just like it was before, you're the only one I've got in this world. The only one!

VII

"Good morning, Bruce." Henrietta put her finger inside the budgie's cage so that he could nibble on it. "Did you sleep well?"

Bruce hopped and pecked at her ring and chirped, "Pretty." She removed his water and food dishes, stepped around the still-sleeping sheep dog, Hector, and carried the dishes into the kitchen for filling. She found Ingrid there, preparing breakfast while giving orders to her cousin Karl, who was readying a turkey for roasting. Cousin Karl was a stocky young man with stoic expression. Henrietta wasn't sure what he did when not working as he did on and off for the Lake household, but he seemed, well, not retarded but not quick, certainly not quick.

"Anyone else up yet?" Henrietta inquired. She hoped not; she'd gotten up early anticipating solitude.

"That Mr. Jones, he's having coffee out on the terrace." Ingrid beat furiously at a pancake mixture in a big bowl. She didn't sound especially happy, but then she never did.

"I wonder what got him up so early." Bruce's containers replenished, Henrietta picked them up carefully so as not to spill anything.

"He said he wanted a swim, but I told him Thor was vacuuming the pool; he'd have to wait until he finished."

"Well, if anyone wants me, I'll be in the garden." And Henrietta finished her bird cage keeping, left the house by

the french doors off the library rather than the dining room
where sliding doors led to the pool. Followed by Hector and
Dorothy, who'd appeared from nowhere, she went out to
the garden toolhouse where she collected gloves, trowel,
kneeling pad and set to weeding, a never-ending job.

An hour or so later, she collected some greens from the
salad garden and took them to the kitchen. The guests were
astir, apparently; Ingrid was setting covered dishes on a Salton
hot tray while instructing Karl on the fine art of serving, a
story he'd heard a hundred times over no doubt. Henrietta,
washing her hands at the kitchen sink, sighed. This day had
begun and must get over and tomorrow would be another
and in the afternoon Attorney Benson would come and hopefully then they'd all go away.

Except Kohinoor. When, Henrietta wondered, would she
leave? Surely she wouldn't stay on indefinitely out here in the
country. Kohinoor was a city girl, a bright-lights person. Not
that she'd been especially difficult, but Henrietta thoroughly
enjoyed, in fact relished, being alone. She had her friends—
Bruce, Dorothy, Hector. And her gardens. And her home.
What else did she need? Nothing.

Henrietta went into the breakfast room. Jason Jones was
there, dressed but damp-haired, he must have had his swim;
Delilah was buttering a muffin, nearly dragging the sleeve of
her ornate caftan in the butter dish; and, surprise, Kohinoor,
hair skinned back in a ponytail giving her a youthful, vul-
nerable look, sat sipping coffee.

"Good morning. I hope you all slept well." Henrietta took
her place at the head of the table.

"Never better." Jason Jones touched his lips with his nap-
kin, smiled. He had marvelous teeth. "I've had a swim. I
feel like a million."

Delilah swallowed the last of her muffin. "Mosquitos," she said. "In my room. I scratched all night."

Henrietta felt her eyebrows rise—mosquitos?—brought them down. "I'll ask Ingrid to spray. We're not usually bothered by mosquitos."

Delilah reached for another muffin. No wonder she seemed a little paunchy; it wasn't all just age. "Bugs love me," she declared flatly, almost proudly. "No matter where I am, they find me. I have sensitive skin."

"Would you mind, Henrietta, if I went into town this morning?" Kohinoor asked indifferently. Why that tone of voice, Henrietta wondered in sudden exasperation, as though she were a child and Henrietta her mother?

"Why not?" Henrietta reached for toast and bacon; she never ate much at breakfast.

For some unexplained reason Kohinoor blushed. "I thought —something to take my mind off—I thought I'd get some yarn and do some needlework."

"It's Sunday," Henrietta reminded her.

"I know, but they have it at that new drugstore. They have everything there."

Delilah regarded Kohinoor. "I never had the patience for that sort of thing. What will you do? A pillow that says 'Take it off'?"

Kohinoor blushed again, ignored the taunt. "I'll find some kind of kit. They have very pretty ones, pieces you can frame."

"Could I hitch a ride with you?" asked Jason. "I'd like to pick up some reading matter. I assume this drugstore has paperbacks?"

"We have rather a full library," Henrietta put in.

"But no thrillers." He grinned at her. "My tastes run to Ian Fleming and Mickey Spillane."

Henrietta had to smile back. "I'm afraid we get no more daring than Agatha Christie."

Kohinoor looked down at her plate. "Won't Pandora"— she was having trouble finding a phrase—"miss you? I don't plan to be back before lunch."

Jason laughed. "Pandora is a sleeper. Noontime's her usual getting-up hour, if not after. She only got up yesterday because of the funeral services; she won't even know I've gone."

"Gone? Where are you going?" Dawn came in on his last sentence. Such a pale young woman, Henrietta thought. A moon maiden.

Kohinoor brushed a strand of hair back. She doesn't want any more passengers, Henrietta thought. I wonder if she's really going for needlework?

Jason drained his coffee cup, set it down. "Into town. For supplies. Frivolous supplies. I take it we're ready to go?" This to Kohinoor.

"If you are. Does it matter which car?" she asked Henrietta.

"Not to me."

Dawn sat down, reached for juice. "Have fun."

"Doing what?" was Don's entrance line. Henrietta remembered when they were little, dressed—or, rather, overdressed —by their proud mother, eternally on display. Now they wore their casual and unalike clothes with definite style. They must be—thirty? About that, Henrietta calculated. Neither had married. Well, that was all right, neither had she. Never considered it, she'd seen enough changes of partners. And Delilah and Aileen, they'd never remarried after divorcing Harry either. Once with Harry was enough? Probably.

Kohinoor escaped, followed by Jason, and Don began to make inroads into food. Dawn, on the other hand, nibbled. Henrietta thought that odd; she believed alcoholics were non-eaters. They talked to each other, almost a foreign language, decided on a swim. Delilah, smoking a cigarette, sat staring. Thinking of what? She was beginning to look her age, Henrietta thought. Definitely. Although she was only three years older than Henrietta. How awkward that had been when Delilah, aged twenty-one, had married Harry and inherited a stepdaughter aged eighteen. Even though only three years separated them, she could pass now as Henrietta's mother. At least, so Henrietta thought. Even with the make-up. Delilah cared so about her looks, while with Henrietta it really didn't matter. When she'd been young, she looked older than her age and now that she was nearly fifty, she looked, maybe thirty-five, prematurely gray? She'd simply stopped looking older somewhere along the line. Fair enough. To make up for other things.

Don and Dawn left, for bathing suits presumably, squabbling about something as they went. They'd fought a lot as children, Henrietta remembered, each vieing for attention. Strange, how they were apparently inseparable. Some people liked to argue; she didn't, abhorred it. But that didn't mean one rolled over and played doggie either. Be patient, use a reasonable tone of voice.

"Henny, are you sure the will hasn't been changed?" Delilah, alone with her, now interrupted her thoughts.

Henrietta frowned. "The will? Changed? Oh, I don't think so. I'm pretty sure not. I mean, Harry would have told me if he'd planned to change it. And Mr. Benson hasn't been here."

Delilah relaxed visibly. "I wasn't sure—I mean, he was generous when we were divorced and I thought he might have changed his mind."

Henrietta tried to pour coffee from the pot, found it empty, rang for more. "Harry had a unique theory, at least it seems unique to me. He earned a great deal of money in his lifetime, some of it before these horrendous income taxes, and then he inherited from my mother and from Audrey. He considered himself the paterfamilias and he thought of all of us, wives and children, as his family. He should have been a sheik or a Mormon. Anyway, he was pleased that he could care for all of us while alive and even after."

Delilah's mouth twisted. "Money. He could give money, so easy; he had plenty of that."

As Henrietta watched, the still-handsome face contorted, quickly tightened into its normal expression of slight discontent. Good heavens, thought Henrietta, she's still in love with him. How peculiar.

They were silent while Karl returned with fresh coffee. Henrietta poured more into both cups, asked, "Are you making a new film?"

Delilah patted a wisp of silver-gold hair back into place. "I've been turning down scripts left and right. Just last week, they wanted me to play an adulterous old woman who seduced her own nephew. A ghastly story—this new trend toward ugliness I find so depressing. There was even a scene where she removed her robe, wearing nothing under it. I told them never, never in a million years."

Henrietta, keeping a straight face, suggested, "Sounds as though it might have been an interesting part. Aside from the nudity."

"Oh, that wasn't all that was wrong. It was an amateurish script and the producer is one of those shoestring boys. It was so much nicer when only the studios were producing. One knew where one stood."

"Good morning." Aileen, clad in beige slacks and matching shirt, with the same color pullover tied across her shoulders, looked like an ad from *Vogue*, Henrietta thought. It must be nice to be so thin, no weight problems; lately she'd been puffing up around the waist, her dresses fit more snugly. Maybe they'd shrunk? Fat chance. Hah, a pun.

"The pancakes are cold, Aileen. I'll get some more for you."

Aileen raised slim brows. "Good heavens, Henny, no! I'm black coffee and cigarettes; Adam says that's a whore's breakfast. Is he down yet?"

"I haven't seen him."

Delilah got up. "I think I'll sit out in the sun by the pool." Henrietta supposed Delilah still resented Aileen; after all, she had been her successor.

"Don't stay too long," Aileen called sweetly after her. "Too much sun causes wrinkles, takes out the natural oils." She made a face at Henrietta. "I'm nasty, aren't I? Just because I'm younger."

Not that much younger, thought Henrietta. "How have you been?" she asked politely. "I haven't had a chance to ask. Very busy, I presume."

A quick puff on Aileen's cigarette, "Yes. Everything's fine. Thank you."

"Is Adam due to graduate this year?"

"He was supposed to, but—he's taking a couple of summer courses."

That meant, Henrietta deduced, that Adam had messed up somewhere. He'd been rather a dreadful little boy as she recalled—horribly spoiled. He was handsome, of course, and bright. Of all of them, he looked most like Harry.

Henrietta heard the telephone ringing in the hall, heard Thor answer it. He came to the breakfast door a moment later, said, "Miss Henrietta, a Mr. Keltie is calling, asking to speak to Mrs. Keltie."

"Good heavens." Henrietta didn't know whether to be

amused or appalled. Bernard Keltie, Pandora's ex-husband, could be a trial. "She isn't up yet. I'll take it."

And she went to the phone, said, "This is Henny, Bernie. Pandora's not up yet. Can I take a message?"

"I just got back from Canada." Bernie's voice was a booming one. "And I read about Harrington. God, I'm sorry I missed the funeral. I was up in the wilds fishing."

"It's kind of you to call."

"I thought I'd drive out today and pay my respects."

"I see . . . well——"

"I should be there by lunchtime. Tell Pandora, will you? Tell her to get her butt out of the sack."

"All right, Bernie. We'll expect you." There'd never been any putting off of Bernard Keltie; one said, "All right, Bernie," because nothing else got through. There'd been an awful row when he and Pandora split up. Henrietta wondered how Bernie and Jason would mix. Oil and water? Or, something more explosive?

She went back to the breakfast room where she found Aileen standing, staring out the bow window toward the pool. "Adam must have decided to skip breakfast," she told Henrietta without looking around. Glancing past Aileen, Henrietta could see Adam, dressed for swimming, on the pool edge.

"No wonder he's so well developed," she murmured. "Guess who's coming to lunch?"

Aileen, cigarette and coffee cup in hand, turned, asked, "Who?" as though she hardly cared.

"Bernard Keltie."

"Good God," Aileen gave an exaggerated shudder. "I thought he'd flown to the ends of the earth."

"Well, he's back and full of sympathy. I've got to tell Ingrid there'll be one more for lunch. What time is it?"

Aileen glanced at her wrist watch, a typically Aileen time-piece, simple but elegant, without hands, only numbers telling the hour. "Just past ten."

"I'd better wake Pandora." Henrietta took a last sip of coffee, ugh, cold. "She'll need time to get used to the idea. Why don't you join the others at the pool, Aileen?"

"I didn't bring a suit." Aileen put her cup down, mashed out her cigarette. "I think I'll go for a walk."

"Go through the gardens, they're especially lovely right now."

"Ummm. Maybe I will."

Ingrid grumbled at Henrietta's news and Pandora swore. "That idiot! What does he want here?" She was sitting up in bed, one strap of her azure lace gown slipped down over one shoulder, hair wrapped in a matching nylon scarf.

"He says he wants to pay his respects."

"Hah! His respects. A fine lot of respect he showed me. . . . Where's Jason? Tell him we'll go into town for lunch. I'm simply not up to Bernard. Any intelligent human being would have more sense than to crash a family gathering at a time like this."

"Jason's already gone to town."

Pandora pulled the slipped shoulder strap back into place. "Why on earth would he do that? So early?"

"He said he wanted to get some mysteries to read."

Pandora made a face. "That's all he reads. Half the time he won't even talk to me, nose in some whodunit." She pushed herself up, sat on the edge of the bed, and groaned. "When did he leave?"

"Maybe a half hour or so ago."

"He should return soon then. I'll just tell him he'll have to drive me back."

Henrietta handed her her robe, it matched her gown,

watched her thrust her feet into ornate slippers. Her toenails were varnished. "I don't think he'll be back as soon as that. Kohinoor said about noon."

Pandora, arms extended to slip into the negligee sleeves, frowned. "What does she have to do with it?"

"He rode in with her." Pandora's scowl was a particularly unattractive one, Henrietta thought, a cleft between the eyes.

It deepened now. "The bastard!" The pampered face twisted. "The miserable, ungrateful, lousy damned bastard!"

Henrietta went to the door. "If you're planning on break-fast, you'd better hurry. Ingrid's an ogre when it comes to regular mealtimes." And she went out, closing the door gently, thought of a long-forgotten strain of music and began to hum as she descended the stairs.

VIII

Bernard Keltie had to cash a check to get to Connecticut, and he picked a gas station out of his bailiwick because he figured it would take maybe seven days counting next weekend to get back to his bank, and then maybe it wouldn't bounce. The gas station owner was one he dealt with in business else he wouldn't have cashed it for Bernie, and even with that edge, the guy wasn't crazy about the idea. "I still got all of Sunday to go," he said. "What if I run out of cash before tomorrow?"

"Listen, Ed, you can do it. All anybody uses is credit cards any more, anyway. And you'd be doing me a big favor that I can repay you for one day. Maybe the next tire order . . ." Bernie was a wholesale tire salesman. Commission only.

"Yeah, well . . ." Ed punched the cash register, slowly began to count out the money. "I've been wanting to talk to you about that. Everybody wants steel-belted radials."

Bernie slapped him on the back. "Hell, man, we got those. Why didn't you say so? I figured they cost too much for your clientele."

Bills in hand, Jeez, the guy moved slow. "Well, I'm kind of overstocked right now on the wide tracks."

"I'll tell you what, Ed"—for God's sake hand over the dough, is a couple of hundred bucks that precious—"I'm going to be away for a couple of days. When I get back, I'll come in and we'll talk about taking them back, replacing them with whatever you got in mind."

"But you told me the last time you didn't accept any turn-backs."

Another slap on the back. "So I can do a little favor for a friend, can't I?"

Ed's saturnine face brightened. "I'd appreciate that, Keltie. I really would. This is a small operation, you know, and when I got a big piece of change tied up in something I can't sell . . ."

Bernie grinned his close-the-deal grin. "Don't you worry, old buddy. We'll take care of that little matter." And so, at last, he had the money. Gas he could buy on credit card, but he couldn't show up at the Lake's without scratch. Pandora, that witch, would know it right off, put him down in front of that snobby crowd; he supposed they were all there, vultures waiting to pick the remains. Suppose he got Pandora to go out to dinner or something and no lettuce to cover the check. He gunned his Cadillac Coupe de Ville, only three hundred payments to go, ha, ha, and roared off down the highway.

Well, he was right. They were all there. Pandora, God, she looked great, fantastic—he'd been a first-class jerk to let her get away; and Henrietta, of course, God, she looked her age; and Delilah, that one could freeze you with a look; and Aileen, that one had some kind of problem, he could smell it and it smelled like her beautiful baby boy Adam, but Bernie couldn't put his finger on what kind of trouble.

And Delilah's two sourballs, Don and Dawn—they sounded like hair-care products or fancy soaps or something and they were some breed of cat he didn't understand at all.

In addition, it turned out, there was some smouldering s.o.b. named Jason Jones that Bernard pegged pretty quick as Pandora's new toy, and—well, well, well—the grieving widow. Now there was something built to fit a queen-size mattress; old Harrington must have had to go some to keep that one happy; who would have thought it? The sly, anemic old dog. No wonder he kicked the bucket.

Pandora sure didn't act glad to see him and the others, for the most part, acted like he was some kind of tramp that wandered in off the street. Except for Henrietta, of course, she'd always been decent. And the widow, she was polite enough. He sat next to her at lunch; a little something to whet the appetite, she was. "Is that your real name, Kohinoor? That's a funny kind of name. Your folks Indian or something?"

She looked at him with those big green eyes and told him her real name was Virginia and truthfully, she said, she'd rather be called Virginia. Kohinoor was her professional name, she went on to explain; perhaps he had heard of the exotic dancer, Kohinoor Diamond?

Well, he hadn't, but he wasn't going to admit that; only before he got a chance to say anything, Adam Lake from across the table grinned like a dog eating taffy and said, "When this is all over, Kohinoor, maybe you'll come out of it with enough bread to open up your own massage parlor. Wouldn't that be neat? All the fellas could come visit."

A nasty crack, that, Bernie was about to tell him so when the widow burst into tears and Jason Jones told Aileen that her son was "surely majoring in bratsmanship" at college, whereupon Pandora lit into Jones and reminded him he wasn't family, to mind his own business, and the widow, sobbing, left the table.

Bernard went after her. He'd heard all that in-fighting before; the Lakes seemed to enjoy it like coyote pups; they played a game of bite until it hurts and somebody squeals his head off. Once Bernard had gone with Pandora to a dude ranch and seen coyotes do that, had thought right off of the Lakes.

Kohinoor sat on the terrace, daubing her eyes with a tissue

and sniffling. "Don't take it to heart, Virginia," Bernard told her. "That's just the way they carry on."

"Yes," Jason Jones spoke from behind Bernard, "they're a pale imitation of a lesser branch of the Borgia family. No poison, just the fangs."

Kohinoor looked up at him, startled. "Poison? What did you say about poison?"

He smiled. "Just a feeble attempt at historic allegory. Sit down, Bernard, the three of us—the outsiders—must band together in these interesting times. Did you ever hear of the Chinese curse, May you live in interesting times?"

Kohinoor gave a final sniffle. "I don't understand you, but I know you're a nice guy. You, too, Mr. Keltie. All right, Bernard, can I call you Bernie? You see, they hate me because of Harrington. They don't think I'm good enough for him— was good enough." At the past tense, new tears wet the wide eyes. "Well, I haven't had all their advantages. My folks died and I had a kid sister to take care of and I had no training at anything but I had to go to work. So I learned how to dance and I'm pretty good at it. I get as much as five hundred dollars a week at some of the better clubs I dance at, and you don't get that kind of money if you aren't good."

"Of course not," murmured Jones. He was lying back in a chaise longue, eyes closed to the sun. A good-looking so-and-so, thought Bernie, slim but all muscles, probably the kind of guy who played handball at some fancy gym. And his clothes, well, maybe it wasn't the clothes. They looked simple, just a plain tan sports shirt and pants just a little lighter in color but on him they looked great. Bernard had always envied a man who could wear clothes. Somehow his shirt was always bunched around his waist and all the pants he ever found were either too big in the rear or too long in the crotch or something.

Nobody was saying anything, so Bernie asked, "Tell us about your kid sister, Virginia. Where is she?"

"Annie's in . . . school." The widow smiled like a little kid. "She's a lot younger than I am, eleven years younger. Momma said Annie was a middle-aged surprise. I tell you, she's beautiful. Her hair is lighter than mine, more of a red-gold, and it's naturally wavy. And she's not as big as I am. I mean, she's really got a beautiful little figure." Kohinoor blushed; Bernie thought that was nice, a woman who could blush like that. "And she's so sweet; there just isn't a sweeter girl on the face of this earth. Sometimes when I go to see her and I see her sitting there all dressed in a pretty pink dress, pink is her favorite color, I could almost eat her, she's so sweet."

Without opening his eyes, Jones said, "When she's out of school, you can bring her here to live with you."

Kohinoor's eyes got even wider. "Here? To this house? But what would Henrietta say?"

Jones opened his eyes to slits. "What will she have to say about it? It will be your house, won't it? You're Harrington Lake's widow."

Kohinoor shook her head emphatically. "Oh, no, it's Henrietta's house. Henrietta explained that to me; it's her home, always has been. She said she's sure Harrington made provision for me in his will, added a codicil is the way she put it, but she made it clear that she's to live here. She said her father promised her that a very long time ago. You see, her mother killed herself in this house."

Jones's eyes were completely open now. He hadn't heard the story. "Her mother killed herself in this house?" He looked back at the house as though it could tell him something.

"Yes, she was Clara Patrick, a very famous movie actress when pictures were silent. I'd never heard of her but Henrietta showed me a book with pictures, press clippings, like a scrapbook. She was a little bit of a thing with blond curls and a heart-shaped face and cupid-bow lips; she looked like a little doll. Well, she was Harrington's first wife and Henrietta's mother, and after Henrietta was born, her mother killed herself. Harrington didn't tell me this, you see, but Henrietta did. I don't know which room she died in; Henrietta didn't tell me that." She shivered suddenly. "I hope it wasn't my room. It's bad enough to be in there after Harrington . . ." Her voice trailed off. Bernard remembered being a kid and having to listen to ghost stories in pitch blackness; Kohinoor sounded like that had felt.

"Why did she kill herself?" Jones wanted to know.

"I'm not sure about that. Henrietta said something about postnatal depression. I guess that means she was unhappy after the baby was born. I don't understand that at all. If I had a baby, I'd be very happy. That's the way I feel about Annie, you know. As though she were my own child."

"She must be a pretty big child by now." Jones got up from the chaise longue, readjusted his shirt at the belt line with one quick motion. "You said you were thirty-one; she must be twenty."

"Yes, she is. But—to me she's still like a little girl." Kohinoor got up, too. "I'm going upstairs. They'll be out soon and I don't feel like seeing them. Thank you, Jason; thank you, Bernie. For being so nice."

IX

"There," said Henrietta to Dorothy on Monday morning. "Somehow we got through the weekend!"

Dorothy blinked up at her from beneath a *Dieffenbachia* bush. Henrietta arose from the larkspur bed she'd been weeding, brushed off her knees, rubbed soil from her hands. The others would be rising; she'd best go bathe and dress. Richard Benson was due just after lunch. She'd invited him to lunch with them but he'd begged off, and she guessed that even Pandora would be getting up earlier than usual this will-reading morning. And then, the reading over, they would go, scatter like the maple leaves in November and she'd be alone again, at last, with Dorothy and Bruce and Hector for company, and good company they were. Even though they were natural enemies, they didn't bicker.

Bicker! Henrietta, in her shower, made a face at the memory of the past two days and got soap in her eyes for her face-making. Pandora had been a witch yesterday with Bernard just because he was Bernard and with Jason just because she was Pandora and Jason was kind to Kohinoor. But then she'd done a complete about-face and insisted that Bernie stay the night, which he did, of course. Bernie never needed much persuading when it came to that sort of thing and when Pandora wanted to turn on the sugar, she could send his sap rising. Sap rising, thought Henrietta smiling, another pun.

Later Delilah and Aileen had had words, while Adam

paired at intervals with either Don or Dawn in a sort of "let's gang up on the other" game. And Don drank a lot. A great deal.

As for Kohinoor, she'd spent most of her time in her room, presumably crying. She was quite adept at that, it seemed, but at least she'd given little trouble if one didn't count Ingrid who'd grumbled a good bit at the number of trays Karl and Hilda had taken up to that room over the past couple of days.

But—she dried briskly with one of her special towels, very thick, very soft, very expensive—Henrietta could take comfort from the fact that it was almost over. Play peacemaker at breakfast and lunch and then, good-by, my fancies!

Only, they were all strangely quiet at breakfast. All faces prepared—men shaven, women made up according to their own taste. Shined and polished, beautiful people this beautiful morning. Polite—"Pass the sugar, please, Kohinoor," and, "Would you care for more coffee, Jason?" Yes, thought Henrietta, we're a lovely lot when we want to be. Adam even held Kohinoor's chair for her when they left the table. And, glory be, lunch was more of the same. Their best behavior. Santa Claus was coming?

Richard Benson was prompt. A contemporary of Henrietta's, he was dressed for the part of family counselor, blue-gray suit with vest, striped tie, and complementary shades of blue.

The will was bound in blue, too, and was a rather thick document by the looks of it. Henrietta hadn't seen it in years, but she didn't recall its being that bulky. Codicils, she assumed. When a man had three living wives (or ex-wives as the case might be) and five children, there were bound to be changes.

Richard Benson was, thankfully, a lawyer who got directly

to the point. Sitting behind the great mahogany desk in the library, he folded back the blue cover. "The original document was filed in 1923 at the time of Harrington Lake's marriage to the late Clara Patrick Lake," Benson began. "In the ensuing years, Mr. Lake was careful to keep his will current, therefore alterations and amendments were made at intervals, the last codicil was filed immediately following his recent marriage to Virginia Klineschmidt Lake."

Everyone looked at Kohinoor. Henrietta, watching the others, thought she could read resentment behind the expressionless faces of the family members. Jason Jones looked amused for a moment, then politely interested; Bernard Keltie smiled encouragingly at Kohinoor.

"Therefore," Benson went on, "rather than reading the original and all its codicils, I've prepared a resume outlining the various bequests." He looked down at a sheet clipped to the end of the sheaf. "To my son Adam Patton Lake, I bequeath the sum of twenty thousand dollars and the hope that he will put his not inconsiderable mental powers to good use. This relatively small bequest is not due to a lack of regard on my part, but to the belief that some people need money more than others and some people know how to use money better than others. Furthermore, in some instances, absolute money like absolute power can corrupt absolutely."

Now it was Adam's turn to be scrutinized. There were red spots on his cheeks and Henrietta saw his eyes flash before he looked away.

"To my son Donald Harrington Lake and to my daughter Dawn Heap Lake, I bequeath the sums of fifty thousand dollars each. I have designated these larger amounts to them because they are older than Adam, their lives are seemingly set, and their futures not so promising."

Dawn started to say something, clamped her mouth tightly

shut. Don's face paled discernibly. They didn't glance at one another but Henrietta guessed they were silently communicating; they'd always been able to do that.

Benson coughed delicately. "To my former wife Aileen Patton Lake, I bequeath the sum of fifty thousand dollars with the admonition that she use the money for herself and herself alone. With this amount and her modeling agency, she should be able to live quite comfortably. But if she is in any way foolish with her bequest, she will, I fear, have to work very hard for a very long time. In the event that I haven't made myself clear, Aileen, do not underwrite Adam in any of his schemes. He is possibly the most clever of all of us and, if forced to, can amount to something."

Aileen, hands clasped tightly in her lap, licked her lips. Adam muttered something beneath his breath.

"To my former wife Delilah Heap Lake, I bequeath——" Benson coughed again, reached for a glass of water Henrietta had placed with pitcher on the desk top. Delilah, sitting very straight, might have been carved from pale, pale marble. "I bequeath to Delilah Heap Lake," Benson read without emotion, "the sum of one hundred thousand dollars. She has been, and still is, a most capable performer but she is getting older and parts for aging leading ladies of Delilah's ilk become scarce. Furthermore, I believe that she has been somewhat unwise in managing her own earnings and, therefore, I bequeath this amount with the following conditions: It shall be kept in trust for her. Attorney Benson will explain the details of the trust, and if properly managed it should provide at least ten thousand per annum which may not keep her in the style to which she is accustomed but will assure her that she need not end up in the Screen Guild Home for Needy Artists."

Watching the actress at work, still playing the role of

statue, Henrietta thought, My, my, he's managed to be generous and insulting in one breath. Harry, you old devil!

"To my daughter, Pandora Lake Keltie . . ." Pandora, listening intently, had her lower lip between her teeth, a mannerism Henrietta recognized from childhood. When faced with the prospect of obtaining favor, or disfavor, from her father, Pandora had worn that very expression. ". . . I bequeath the sum of two hundred thousand dollars . . ."—Pandora exhaled softly—"but under the same arrangement as the bequest to Delilah." Pandora stiffened. "My daughter Pandora is perhaps the most insecure of all of us. She plays like the grasshopper not only in summer but the whole year long. The interest on her trust should provide some twenty thousand a year and to this I add the house on the Riviera where she can live in comparative high style on this, to her, small amount of income."

Pandora glanced at Henrietta; Henrietta recognized the look. It said, You see how he hates me! You were always his favorite! Then Pandora looked at Jason Jones, but his head was tilted downward. Henrietta felt a momentary pity for her half-sister. But only momentary, Pandora earned her wages.

"And to my beloved daughter Henrietta . . ." Henrietta was abruptly wary. She should have come last—and the first shall come last—but Kohinoor had not yet been mentioned. What did this mean, that he'd left nothing to Kohinoor? But no, that couldn't be. Mr. Benson had said the last codicil was made after the marriage. Could Kohinoor have disappointed him in some way? What did it mean?

"And to my beloved daughter Henrietta, I bequeath the sum of five hundred thousand dollars which she, wise in the ways of investment and careful in her living habits, can use as she sees fit."

Henrietta waited for the rest, the house that was hers, that had been promised to her since childhood. It looked now as though he would leave the rest, a considerable amount to Kohinoor, but that was all right, five hundred thousand and the house would do very nicely; Henrietta wasn't greedy.

"And last but not least, to my dear wife, Virginia Klineschmidt Lake, I bequeath the rest of my estate, real and personal, including stocks, bonds, and real estate. As I stated previously, various people have various needs and I shall rest in peace knowing that my dear wife shall need never to return to her previous profession and that her every wish shall be granted. Her early life was a struggle. She was valiant and she was a joy to me in my autumn years. Thus, for value and virtue, Virginia, my dear, the reward."

He's given her my house, thought Henrietta. How could he do that? He's given her my house.

"Does that mean . . . ?" Kohinoor's voice was weak. "How much money do I . . . I mean . . ."

Mr. Benson regarded her soberly. "It means, my dear Mrs. Lake, that you are a woman of considerable property, or will be as soon as this instrument is probated. All things considered, in the neighborhood of three million dollars."

Kohinoor stared at him.

"And in the event that any of the legatees herein mentioned should die before this will is executed, his or her legacy shall be divided among the survivors," Benson read on. "I exclude, however, from this condition the bequest to Virginia Klineschmidt Lake. Should she die prior to the execution of this will, her share shall go to various charities I have listed with my attorney. And I advise her to make her own will promptly."

There was silence. Then a chair scraped; who moved? Richard Benson stood up.

"Tell me again," Kohinoor spoke. "I'm not sure I heard you right the first time. I'm rich? This is my house now?"

"That's correct." Was the look Benson gave her one of sympathy?

Kohinoor bounced up from her chair and clapped her hands. "Then I can bring Annie here! I'll have a home for Annie!"

When Benson had gone, attaché case in hand, and Kohinoor had taken herself up to her room to cry for joy, or do whatever a newly rich widow would do, Henrietta called an impromptu conference of family. She hadn't minded Jason and Bernard being present for the will reading, and Pandora, for some Pandora-ish reason had wanted them there, but she told them now, "I'm sure you'll understand." Bernard, who knew her rather well, and Jason, who knew her not well at all, thought she looked peculiar. The two men moved out to the terrace by the pool where Jason, sitting on the parapet that separated pool from patio mused, "The old man was generous, but I'll bet Pandora's fit to be tied."

Bernard, thinking of a house on the Riviera and twenty thousand guaranteed dollars a year, sighed. "She'll manage somehow. Pandora always does."

"Yes, I imagine she will." Jason lit a cigarette with a fancy-looking lighter and looked at his watch. Bernard thought that was a watch that had cost a pretty penny. "What's the best way to get back to New York?"

"By car, or taxi, but that costs an arm and a leg. There's a bus from town, but I don't guess you'd go for that. Are you planning on taking off right away?"

"I think I should go as soon as possible. I wouldn't want to outstay my welcome and I've been neglecting my business."

"Which is . . . ?"

Jason smiled coolly. "I have a number of investments."

I'll bet you do, thought Bernie. "Pandora going with you?"

"I shouldn't think so. I imagine she'll be flying off to her little gray home on the Mediterranean."

"Then you're not going along?"

Jason put on his smile again. "I think not. Doubt if I'm even invited." He stood, brushed at his impeccable trouser legs. "I believe I'll go up and pack. Someone may be driving into the city and I'll want to be ready if they'll take me along."

"Yeah. I guess I should be going, too. Only I go north to New England." Yet Bernie remained where he was, staring down at the sparkling turquoise waters of the pool, wondering, trying to imagine what Pandora and Henrietta and the rest of them were talking about inside the house and thinking, too, that he really would be pretty dumb to take off now. Now, when Pandora might need him. Maybe he'd just hang around and see what happened.

"It's intolerable," Pandora fumed, "absolutely intolerable. I can't imagine what got into him."

"Harrington was a romantic. Unfortunately, he fell in love again. If he'd lived longer, he would have changed his mind and added yet another codicil." Aileen sounded drained. "I don't envy her a share, but such an unfair share."

"Share!" Delilah's tone was bitter. "I'd say she got the cake, we got the crumbs. What are you doing, Don? Can't you stay away from the liquor in a time of crisis?"

"I thought I'd toast the victor." He laughed harshly. "You know, to the victor belongs the spoils."

"What are we going to do?" asked Dawn.

"Yes, Henrietta, say something. What are we going to do? Can't we contest this ridiculous will? Can't we take her to court? What are we going to do?" Pandora's face was flushed and her hair was mussed, very un-Pandora.

"I'll tell you what we can do," Adam spoke up from the depths of the chair he slumped in, chin on chest, legs stretched full length in front of him. "We can claim she knew all about the will and set her up for doing in dear old Father."

"Adam!" His mother looked at him in horror.

"We'd never get away with that," muttered Don.

"How do we know she didn't know?" demanded Dawn. "How do we know she didn't kill him. Dr. Henderson is an old fuddy-duddy."

"You're not serious . . . ?" Delilah sounded as though she were reading a new play and wasn't quite sure of her lines.

"Who says we're not serious?" Adam grinned.

"I say you're not." Henrietta had been staring out the window at her gardens. Now she turned to face them, eyes calm, expression serene. "In the first place, it wouldn't work. He was cremated, remember? That gives nothing to go on, no corpse to be exhumed, no autopsy."

"All the better," said Adam. "If we can't prove she did, she can't prove she didn't."

Henrietta gave him one look. "Harry was right about you," she murmured. "You must learn to use your brains. Now I shall tell you what we're going to do; we're going to make the best of it, that's what we're going to do. Harry made his wishes known and we all know Harry always had his way. So we shall simply accept his decisions. He has judged us, so be it."

"You can accept if you like, but personally I'm going to see a lawyer," Pandora looked petulant. "A good lawyer," she amended. "There must be some basis to break this will—undue influence, something."

"My dear Pandora, Kohinoor was his wife. Furthermore, he didn't leave us exactly penniless." Henrietta thrust her hands into the pockets in her skirt. "I say we shall be kind to her. I say we shall accept her in the family. We'll do whatever we can to help her. In short, we shall act like the civilized human beings we are, rather than a pack of animals. Think of the dreadful publicity, the Lake family squabbling over the Lake money. Think what it would do to all your reputations. No, we'll be kind. Kind and patient."

"I don't care——" began Pandora.

"Sister Pandora"—Adam made the phrase a near insult—"listen to big sister Henrietta. And cool it. What she's saying is, there's more than one way to skin a pussycat."

They all looked at Henrietta. Finally, Aileen said, "What will you do, Henny? This house—you love it so."

"I expect Kohinoor will permit me to stay on for a while until I can find another place to live."

"Who's this Annie she was talking about?" Dawn asked.

"Her younger sister, I believe," Henrietta told them. "She's mentioned her to me a time or two. She's still in school, I think. Much younger than Kohinoor, maybe twenty or so."

Adam grinned a Cheshire grin. "Froggy may a-courtin' go." He pushed himself up in the chair. "Marry the Lake money? Why not?"

"Adam, what a thought." Aileen looked shocked. "It would be like marrying one of the family."

"Incest, Mama? Say not so. No relation. None at all. Besides"—he slid back down—"I was only funnin'."

"She probably wouldn't have you," was Dawn's opinion. "Not if she's got any sense."

"How about me?" asked Don.

"You're too old," Dawn snapped.

"I wasn't thinking of baby sister. I was thinking of the widow lady herself."

Dawn looked aghast. "You're kidding."

"Am I?" They exchanged twin looks.

"We've got to go back to the city," Dawn reminded him. "Do we?"

"I suggest you all stay on for a while," Henrietta counseled. "I suggest you stay on at least until the girl gets here. After all, you should meet her; we all should. Make her welcome."

"But when will that be?" asked Delilah. "I should get back to the coast. There's a script I'm supposed to read; they're waiting on my answer."

"I don't know. Soon, I should think. I mean, how long can it take to take a girl out of school and bring her here?" Henrietta turned back to the window. "I'd feel so much better if you were all here. Not quite so lost."

"You lost?" Pandora's voice rose, was almost gay. "Why, Henny, I never thought I'd see the day. Henrietta lost? Never."

X

Kohinoor stole a glance at the girl beside her in the back seat of the limousine. Annie saw her glance, looked back. "Do you like your new dress?" Kohinoor asked her sister. "You look lovely in it."

"Yes, thank you," answered Annie.

She did look lovely. Her hair was not so red as Kohinoor's, more of an amber gold, and where Kohinoor's hair was heavy and convoluted, Annie's hair grew in small soft curls and was cut, very nicely in a cap around her face, in a shag in the back. And while Kohinoor's eyes were definitely green, Annie's eyes were more of a turquoise tone. Her skin, opposed to the whiteness of Kohinoor's (typical of a redhead), was a golden tan color; she'd been out in the sun and fresh air at the school, playing games no doubt. And there was a sprinkling of golden freckles across her nose.

The new dress she wore was pale pink and it fitted her petite figure perfectly. Kohinoor was proud of her younger sister. The others, the Lakes, would just have to love her as much as she did.

Because Thor was listening in the front seat, if not exactly listening, he could certainly hear, Kohinoor was careful in what she said. "I know it will be hard, meeting so many people at once, confusing," she told Annie. "There's Henrietta, they call her Henny; she's the oldest. She's Harrington's daughter by his first wife. Well, she's not the oldest if you count Delilah—I think Delilah is older than Henrietta. She was Harrington's third wife; the first two died. But I think of Henrietta as being older than Delilah." She thought a moment. "In some ways."

"Henny," said Annie. "Like in Henny Penny. And Delilah. Like in the Bible."

"Yes, that's right. Then Aileen is there; she's Harrington's fourth wife, the one before me. That's all of Harrington's wives, but there are other children. Well, they're not children, of course, but they're Harrington's sons and daughters and Henny's half-brothers and half-sisters. There's Pandora; she's Pandora Lake Keltie because she once married a Bernard Keltie, then divorced him, and he's there, too. I don't know just why he's there; he came for lunch one day and just stayed on. Then there's Don and Dawn Lake, they're twins. And Adam Lake, he's the closest to your age."

"Pandora," said Annie, "like the box with all the troubles in the world."

"Yes," Kohinoor agreed although she couldn't remember that story. "And then, there's Jason Jones, too."

"Jason of the Golden Fleece? Who is he?"

Kohinoor frowned. "I'm not really sure. A friend of Pandora's, I guess. He came from Paris with her."

"Paris, France?"

"That's right. Would you like to go there one day, Annie? We can go now, whenever, wherever we want to."

"Maybe. Who's the man driving this car?"

"Oh, that's Thor. I told you. Thor is the chauffeur." It embarrassed Kohinoor to be talking of Thor as though he weren't there.

"Thor and the hammer," murmured Annie.

Kohinoor, who by now had missed several of Annie's references, didn't know what Thor had to do with a hammer, but then Annie had had a better education than she had. At the school, they'd spoken in glowing terms of Annie's interest in reading. "And you'll meet Thor's wife, Ingrid, she's the cook, and Hilda, she's Ingrid's cousin, I think, and Karl, he's some relation, too."

"Cousin," Thor told them from the front seat. Kohinoor saw him looking at them in the rearview mirror. She thought he'd seemed quite taken with Annie. Well, she was a little beauty, had been born beautiful. Kohinoor could remember when she'd been brought home from the hospital; she'd looked like a little baby doll from the toy department in the big store downtown.

"We're almost there now," Kohinoor told her sister, taking her hand. "This is the long driveway that leads to the house and it's ours, all of it. Our first real home since you were just a baby."

Annie put her face up close to the window so she could see out. She saw the trees and shrubs and the rose garden and the big expanse of front lawn and the house itself, wide and white with a pillared center and two graceful wings, and she said, "Oh, it looks like a palace."

"Well," said Kohinoor, "I guess it is, kind of. A modern-day palace."

Henrietta was waiting for them in the living room. Kohinoor recalled her first impression of Henny. A small, mild woman, with a braided crown of gray hair, neatly dressed in nothing special she could remember, aged somewhere in her middle years. When she introduced Annie to her, Annie asked, "Are you my fairy godmother?"

Henny looked startled for a moment, then held out her hands and said, "I could try to be. Welcome, Annie. Welcome home."

The others, it seemed, were out on the terrace by the

swimming pool. "Swimming pool?" asked Annie. Then, proudly, "I know how to swim."

"Would you like to put your suit on?" asked Henny.

"Yes, I'd like that. Could I, Virginia? Go for a swim?"

"Well, yes, I suppose so. Is Thor bringing the bags up? Yes, I guess he is. I'll take you up to your room—we've picked a special one for you, and we'll find your swim suit."

"It's a new one," Annie told Henrietta. She laughed her tinkling little laugh. "It's called a bikini." She repeated the word, "bikini."

"It sounds very nice," said Henny. "What color is it?"

Annie scowled, tiny lines appeared on her smooth brow. "I've forgotten. We bought so many things. What color is it, Virginia?"

"We bought two," Kohinoor reminded her. "One is white and the other is pink with daisies on it."

"Oh, yes." Now Annie remembered. "I'll wear the one with the daisies."

"I'll tell them you're coming," said Henrietta.

"Yes, do. Tell them I can swim."

"They're here," Henny announced to the group by the pool.

"What's she like?" asked Adam who lay face down on a sun chaise.

"She reminds me of"—Henrietta chose her words carefully —"a very young Norma Jean Baker."

Adam rolled over to look at her. "Who is Norma Jean Baker, for God's sake?"

Delilah answered, "She means Marilyn Monroe." She fell back against the cushions of her chaise, closed her eyes. "I think I smell trouble."

"Not the kind you think," Henrietta told her.

"What do you mean?" asked Pandora.

"I'm not sure what I mean. It could be that she's simply quite immature."

"What do you mean she's simply immature?" was Aileen's question.

"Well, she's—" Henny groped for words—"very wide-eyed, small high voice, very open."

"So?" Dawn, on the pool edge, feet in the water, squinted up at her.

"She says very odd, simple things. She told me to tell you she knows how to swim."

Don, on the diving board, wanted to know, "How old did you say she was?"

"Kohinoor said—twenty."

"What was the name of that school she went to?" asked Pandora.

"Kohinoor said it was Westwood or Crestwood, something like that. In upper New York state."

"You want to check on it?" Bernard offered. "Give me the name of the town and I can find out. I've got connections."

"I'll find out," Henrietta promised. "In the meantime—" she could swear they all leaned forward—"in the meantime, be very nice, very gentle with her."

"Oh," said Adam, "I will. I will."

XI

Virginia had said Annie could have anything she wanted now. "Anything?"

"Yes, anything."

"And I don't have to go back to Crestwood? Never? No matter what?"

"Never. No matter what."

Annie hugged her sister. She thought Virginia hugged harder than she did, too hard, maybe. She slipped out of her grasp. "I want to go swimming again."

"So late? Can't it wait until tomorrow, Annie? It's dark out and they'll be having dinner soon."

"I want to go now. I didn't get to swim very long this afternoon and you bought me those two pretty bathing suits." Already it was happening. They told you, you could do as you pleased and then wouldn't let you.

"Tomorrow will be a better time. Really, Annie. Why don't you put on that pink polka-dot dress I bought you, the one with the long skirt you liked so much, and we'll go downstairs and you can have a ginger ale or a Coca-Cola."

"I want a root beer. Nice and cold."

"Well, I'm not sure we have any root beer, but we'll get some tomorrow."

Annie opened her mouth, then shut it tight. It wasn't any different, not that she could see. Anything she wanted—well, there had been two wants she couldn't have already and it wasn't even dinnertime yet.

"Can you manage by yourself? Your shower and your dress and all?" Virginia sounded a little like old Miss Bilkington when you listened but didn't look at her. Annie had hated old Miss Bilkington worse than anyone else at Crestwood. Virginia shouldn't sound like that.

"Of course I can."

"Then, I'll go get dressed myself. Come to my room when you're ready if you're ready before I am. I'm right next door, remember?"

"Of course I do!" Yes, Virginia definitely sounded like old Miss Bilkington. Something should be done about that. Voice lessons or something. She, Annie, had had voice lessons. She could sing. Her favorite song was "Beautiful Dreamer." She began to hum it in the shower. "Beautiful dreamer, queen of my song, list while I woo thee with sweet melodies."

The pink dress was long and silky. It was her first long dress and it made her feel very grown-up, made her look grown-up, too, she could see by the mirror.

She went to the door, opened it quietly, was old Miss Bilkington sneaking around the hall? Of course not, she wasn't at Crestwood any more. This was home, her new home forever, Virginia had told her. Let's see, which was the way downstairs? Down the hall this way, yes, there were the stairs, wide and curving. She went down them, holding the bannister with one hand and her dress up with the other, and found herself in the big hallway where they'd come in. She could hear voices; she went to find the others. They were sitting in the living room; the rugs were thick and soft to walk on, the lights were nice, too, not too bright; they made everyone look pretty.

"Hello, Annie." It was the young man who greeted her, the one nearest her age. What was his name? Adam. Yes, Adam. The beginning-of-the-world Adam.

"Hello, Adam. Hello, everybody. Do you like my new dress?"

"It's very becoming, Annie." This from Henny Penny; the way she wore her gray hair braided around made Annie think of Mrs. Barnes, the superintendent at Crestwood. "Would you like something to drink?"

"Have you got any——?"

"Let me get you something, Annie. A nice sweet drink with lots of fruit?" Adam stood near the place where the bottles and glasses stood. He smiled at her. She thought he was good-looking, like a picture of Galahad she remembered from a book. "I'll make it pink," he said, "to match your dress."

"All right." This was more like it. Anything she wanted.

"As I was saying, Henny"—the woman with the white-gold hair spoke—"I simply must return to the Coast this weekend. There are business matters that must be taken care of."

"I'm sorry if you must go, Delilah," Henny answered.

"I'm sure Bernie has to go, too." This one was Pandora, Annie remembered her. Annie thought she was the prettiest of them all. There was a kind of shine about her.

Bernie, he was the man who was losing his hair, he was kind of fat, too, he had another name, Bernard, said no, he didn't have to go until he'd worn out his welcome. "I'm my own boss. I can take a vacation when I feel like it."

"Here you are, Princess." Adam handed Annie a tall glass. There was a red cherry on the top. The liquid was pink, as promised, and frothy. She tasted it.

"Ummm. It's good. What is it?"

"A little invention of my own. I'll call it 'the Princess' after you."

"I'm not a princess." Wasn't he nice? She smiled at him over the glass.

"You look like a princess. How do you like your new home?"

She glanced around. "It's all right. Better than Crestwood."

"Crestwood?"

"Yes. That's where I used to live."

"Oh, yes. Your school."

Annie nodded, drank from her glass. It was delicious. And she was thirsty. She drank it right to the bottom, held it out to Adam. "May I have more? Please?"

"Sure." He grinned at her. The thin woman sitting near them looked at him in a funny way.

She asked, "Are you sure, Adam? I don't know if Annie is used to——"

"Now, Mother, dear." The thin woman was his mother. How lucky he was to have a mother. "It's just a harmless little concoction."

"What were you studying at school, Annie?" Dawn, that was this one's name. She was one of the twins; the other one sat next to her drinking something brown from a short glass. Not very sensible to be named Dawn and Don. It sounded the same. They could be Don and Don or Dawn and Dawn if you said it fast.

"Books."

"I beg your pardon?"

"I was studying books and singing and swimming and any-thing else you could think. That's what you do when you're at Crestwood. They try and teach you everything. I guess I learned to do almost everything. Except cook. I'm not very good at that."

Adam laughed. "I don't guess you have to worry about cooking."

"I don't know. It's supposed to be very important. Old Miss Bilkington used to get very cross about it. She said I should at least be able to boil water. That was a silly thing to say, don't you think? I mean, anybody can boil water. You just put it in a pan and turn the heat on."

Adam laughed again, that made her smile, too, and handed her a glass, once again filled with pink froth. This one had two cherries.

"Have you seen Annie . . . ?" Virginia appeared in the doorway. She looked cross, like old Miss Bilkington did sometimes, well, most of the time, to tell the truth. "Oh, there you are, Annie. I thought you were coming to my room, that we were coming down together."

"I found my way." Oh, this pink drink was so delicious. She couldn't stop drinking it.

"What are you drinking?" asked Virginia, her voice rising. To the others she said, "She's not used to alcohol."

"It's just a little cherry heering with grenadine and ginger," Adam told her. "Very mild, very innocent."

"Well, she can't have it. Give me that, Annie. It's not good for you."

Annie clutched her glass tightly. "You said I could have anything I wanted. And you said they didn't have any root beer. So I want this. You said!"

"I think it's time to go in to dinner anyway," said Henny quickly. "Here's Karl to tell us so."

"Come on, Annie." Adam was at her side. He spoke softly, "Maybe we'll go for a swim later on. In the moonlight."

"Oh." She beamed up at him. "I'd like that." They walked out ahead of the others, then Pandora came, followed by Bernard, and Jason put out his hand to Kohinoor and said, "Come along, Virginia. It's not that serious."

She shook her head dumbly but went with him. "She isn't used to . . ." she murmured.

"But she'll have to get used to a lot of things. She's out in the world now. You brought her out."

Head down, voice low, Kohinoor said, "It's what I've always wanted for her. She's entitled to a life, a normal life. She—" she looked at him, there were tears in her eyes—"she just stopped growing. In her mind. The doctors said"—she blinked away the tears—"she's like a very bright ten-year-old. Something went wrong; she was born that way, they said. But she deserves a life."

"Of course she does. And you can give her one." He leaned down to her, "Maybe the best thing would be to get these people away from here."

"But how can I? It was their father's home. And Delilah and Aileen are their mothers, so they're family, too."

Jason shrugged, pulled out her chair for her. "It's your house now," he spoke softly. "Yours and Annie's."

She watched Adam bend over Annie across the table, saw him say something, heard Annie laugh. "Yes," said Kohinoor, "you're right." And when they were all there at the dinner table, she raised her voice. "Listen, all of you, I'm sorry but I want you all to leave. Tomorrow."

They looked at her, blank faces, and Annie started to say something but Henny spoke first. "It's fairly simple for most of us, Kohinoor, but what about me? You said—I could take my time. I have a great many possessions. And there's Bruce and Hector and Dorothy, one just can't take them to a hotel."

"Of all the highhanded arrogance!" Pandora's laser glare could have cut through steel.

"All right." Kohinoor set her jaw. "Henny can stay. A while. But the rest of you—" she looked directly into

Adam's leer—"you go. Annie needs peace and quiet. You go."

Annie eyed Adam from over her pink glass. Kohinoor could almost hear them sending thoughts to one another, there was a hum in the air around them, she could feel it. She could feel the resentment, too, the hatred burning anew, an old cigarette that hadn't gone out. Well, they'd always hated her. Let them hate her a little bit more.

She had Annie to think of.

"I'll take rooms in town"—Jason had a way of using his voice, not a whisper, yet no one else could hear—"in case you need me."

Kohinoor hesitated, then, "That won't be necessary."

Jason shrugged. "Whatever you say."

XII

The sun came up, carelessly throwing its heat around, and Henrietta, out in her garden since an early hour, knew it was going to be an uncomfortable day. She wiped a film of perspiration from her upper lip, took off her gardening hat and gloves, and left them in the potting shed. She went into the house through the kitchen where Ingrid was scowling and frying bacon. "You can tell Karl and Hilda we won't be needing them after today," Henrietta told her. "They're leaving this morning. All except Mrs. Lake and her sister."

"Good riddance," muttered Ingrid.

"Yes," agreed Henrietta. "Good riddance."

She went up to her room, showered, and changed into a blue-and-white-checked cotton frock. She smoothed her hair, put on pale lip rouge. Dorothy was curled up on her bed, asleep. She patted the cat and went down to breakfast.

Delilah was there with the twins. "We're packed," she told Henrietta. "Can Thor drive me to the airport or has that woman given orders that I should walk?"

"Of course Thor can drive you," Henrietta assured her.

"Good." Delilah picked up her coffee cup. "We want to get out of here as soon as possible."

"Amen," Dawn seconded the motion.

Bernard came in, asked, "Where's Pandora? I told her to get up early, I'd drive her down to New York."

"And Jason, too?" asked Dawn blandly.

Bernard frowned. "I don't know where or how he's going. Not with me."

"If you've forgotten anything," Henrietta told Delilah, "we'll send it to you."

"What an outlandish hour of the morning." Pandora appeared in the doorway, clad completely in a soft shade of salmon. With clothes like that, Henrietta reasoned, her annual income would be spent in a month.

"Tell you what"—Bernard grinned at her happily—"I'll take you to lunch at the Plaza."

"With what?" Pandora was not in one of her better moods. "Where's Aileen?" she asked Henrietta. "She said she knew of an apartment for sublet."

"You're planning to stay in New York?" Henrietta was surprised.

Pandora shrugged. "For a while. Until I hear from my friends. They're all over the place. I'll let you know where to forward mail." She assumed an injured look, sat down, and helped herself to coffee. "I'd planned to stay on here a while, until I got my plans set. I can't even stay in my father's house to mourn my own father!"

"He'd be turning in his grave if he knew." Delilah nodded wisely.

"Well, what can you expect?" asked Dawn. "From a woman like that?"

"Must be some kind of mental deficiency in that family." Her brother's voice was muffled by his coffee cup.

"Henny, isn't there something we can do?" Pandora's tone had a whine to it. "All that money in that woman's hands!"

"Good morning, fellow travelers." Adam entered grinning. "Ready for the modern version of *Canterbury Tales*? Too bad we can't all ride off, on donkeys, wearing sackcloth."

"You're in remarkable good humor," Henrietta told him.

"Why not?" He cocked an eyebrow. "You win a few; you lose a few."

"Did you go for your moonlight swim with Cinderella?" Dawn queried.

"Ask me no questions, I'll tell you no lies." His grin widened before he hid it behind a cup.

"You'll get nowhere with that one," was Pandora's opinion. "Besides, how can you stand her? It's like talking to a child."

"Oh, she has her charms."

"If you step out of line and that woman finds out, she'll have you tarred and feathered," Delilah predicted.

"Maybe," said Adam. "Maybe not."

"I'm almost out of gas, I think." Aileen, dressed in a pale pants suit, set her suitcase down in the hall as she entered. "I'll have to get some in the village."

"Where's Jason?" Henrietta wanted to know. "Has he arranged for transportation?"

Pandora shrugged. Oh ho, thought Henrietta without surprise. "He can go in the limousine with Delilah," she reasoned out loud.

Karl appeared from the kitchen, waited for breakfast orders. Nobody, it seemed, was hungry except for Henrietta who ordered her usual four-minute eggs. "Ingrid's cooked a plateful of bacon." Karl looked as though he couldn't understand people who didn't eat breakfast.

"Bring it with toast," Henrietta ordered. She told the others, "You'll have time for that."

"I don't want to see that woman," Delilah protested.

"She's not normally an early riser," said Henrietta.

Pandora pouted. "Neither am I."

"Nor that dreadful girl," Delilah went on.

"I didn't hear her stirring when I was upstairs," Henrietta assured her.

"Adam probably kept her up too late," Dawn snickered.

"I think—" Jason spoke from the doorway, "I think somebody had better call the police."

All heads turned in his direction.

"There's been . . . an accident. Virginia—Kohinoor's in the swimming pool. Floating. Face down. I'm very much afraid she's dead."

XIII

His name was Vincent Prosper and he was a detective, because when the selectmen of the town, especially the first
selectman, got all uptight about crime in the streets and how
it might even come to this town, Chief of Police Bacon had
been persuaded to set up a detective bureau and Vincent was
it. Vincent was it because, although he was fairly new on
the force, only three years, he had attended a community
college for one year and a semester of the second year, and
the first selectman was impressed by a policeman who had
"pursued higher learning."

Most of the time Vincent liked being Detective Prosper,
because he read a lot of murder mysteries and he liked to use
the fingerprint kit and walk around in plain clothes so that
nobody would know he was a detective, only everybody did,
which kind of spoiled things. But not really, because there
wasn't that much to do most of the time.

Only now—with Chief Bacon in the hospital for a gall-
bladder operation and this woman had been murdered—
actually murdered—out at the Lake place, Vincent didn't like
being a detective so very much.

Until he met the girl. Annie Klineschmidt was her name,
a terrible name, hard to spell, but she was the prettiest girl
he'd ever seen in his life and, besides, she trusted him. He
could tell from the way she looked up at him.

It was her sister who had been killed. Hit over the head
with a blunt object, Dr. Henderson had said, and thrown

into the swimming pool. The sister's name had been Virginia Klineschmidt Lake, only other people at the house, most of them Lakes, went around calling her Kohinoor, which was really a terrible name. It seemed she had been a dancer on the stage and that was her stage name, Kohinoor Diamond. Miss Henrietta Lake, Vincent knew her because she'd always lived there, whereas the others used to live there, most of them, but didn't any more, explained that Kohinoor Diamond was some kind of joke like the Grateful Dead or some of those groups and that there really was a Kohinoor Diamond, a great big jewel like the Queen of England had in her crown.

Tom Peevey, he was Officer Peevey and was nearly forty years old and had been a member of the force for so long that he'd developed a bad disposition, snickered when Miss Lake had explained and later expressed an opinion to Vincent that the victim had been nothing but a cooch dancer. When Vincent asked what a cooch dancer was, Tom said, "You know, one of them belly dancers like they have in Egypt and those places."

Be that as it may, the victim had been a good-looking girl in her time, according to Annie, who declared her sister was "beautiful" and had pictures to prove it.

And again, be that as it may, Vincent nodded his head to agree with Annie, even though the victim, when he'd seen her, was not a pretty sight at all, no, not at all; and in his humble opinion Annie was a lot better-looking, a lot, than her sister, even though, admittedly, her sister hadn't been in the best of shape when they'd fished her out of that swimming pool.

"Now, here's the ones that are there," he explained to Chief Bacon who was still flat on his back in the hospital, but "recuperating." "There's this Henrietta Lake, you know her; she's always winning prizes at the garden show. And there's Pandora Lake; her name is Keltie now because she was once married to a guy named Bernard Keltie, only she isn't any more, but he's there, too."

"I remember her," said Chief Bacon feebly. "I was in high school when her mother drowned. Her mother was a big movie star; she sang and danced like Judy Garland. Her name was Audrey Dell."

Vincent didn't comment. He'd never heard of Audrey Dell. "There's a movie star there," he went on, "Delilah Heap. She was once married to Harrington Lake; he sure had a lot of wives. All his children had different mothers except Don and Dawn Lake, they're twins, their mother is Delilah Heap."

Chief Bacon shook his head as though he didn't understand and Vincent had to spell the names Don and Dawn for him. "Then there's another lady who was Mrs. Lake, Aileen Patton Lake is her name and she has a boy, Adam, not much younger than me; he's Harrington Lake's youngest. That's all the family except the victim's sister. And there's this guy named Jason Jones, I don't know just how he fits in. Miss Henrietta Lake says he's Mrs. Keltie's friend."

"I don't know how you keep them straight," Chief Bacon complimented Vincent who was pleased. "It isn't easy," he admitted. "And there's this Ingrid and Thor Helstrum, too, and Ingrid's cousins Hilda and Karl who have been working there, Olson's their last names, while this big bunch was at the house for Harrington Lake's funeral."

"So what have you found out so far?" Chief Bacon tried to push himself up on his pillows, grimaced. He had a lot of stitches, he told Vincent, and what's more, a lot of gas.

Vincent referred to his official notebook. "Well, first of all, all of them were fixing to leave when I got out there, all but Henrietta and Annie, you remember, that's the victim's sister. So the first thing I said was, 'Hold it. You aren't going anywhere till this business is cleared up.'"

"They didn't give you any trouble, did they?" The chief had a paunch to start with and now, maybe from the gas, his sheet stood up on his middle like a little snow-covered mountain.

"No, sir. They might have, but Miss Henrietta Lake was very co-operative. She calmed them all down. They were pretty excited, especially the sister, of course, Annie. She cried and shook all over and Henrietta sat with her arms around her like she was her mother until Doc Henderson gave her something to put her to sleep for a while. While they were doing that, I began to interview the rest of them, one by one. I asked them where they were and what they were doing the night before. I started on that tack because Doc Henderson said it looked to him at first glance, at least, that she'd been in that swimming pool a good part of the night."

"Hand me a cup of that water, will you, Vinnie? And one of them straws that bend. I'm supposed to drink a dozen glasses of water a day or they'll put me on that intravenous again." Vincent obliged, and when the chief had sipped noisily, he asked, "Did you come up with anything you could put your finger on?"

Vincent looked back at his notebook. He wished it could tell him something, but the words on it were pretty pat. "Pandora and that Jones fella, they came into town and spent the evening at the inn in the bar and dining room. I saw them there myself about seven, didn't know who they were then, of course. They looked to be having an argument."

He flipped a page. "Then Aileen Patton Lake and Miss Henrietta Lake and Dawn Lake, the girl twin, and Adam Lake, he's the youngest you remember, they played bridge until nearly midnight; they all said that."

The chief frowned, sucked some more water. "That leaves some out, doesn't it?"

"Yes, sir. Delilah Heap Lake and her son, Don, and Bernard Keltie and the victim's sister, Annie. Don Lake went to bed around eleven; Bernard Keltie said he was blotto, said Don Lake likes the sauce, while Delilah Heap Lake watched television, seems there was an old picture starring her on the TV. I looked it up in yesterday's newspaper. It was on all right. And Bernard Keltie, he went in and played some pool; they've got a regular billiard table with all the fixings, real nice, and Annie watched him for a while, he told me, said she had never seen a pool table before."

"Did Doc Henderson give you the exact time of the killing?"

"Not yet, he didn't. I'm expecting to hear more from him in the A.M. And I've got to make a long distance phone call, Chief. To a man in New York named Richard Benson. He's a lawyer and it seems as though last week he told all of those present just how Harrington Lake split up his property. What he did was, gave them all some, but he gave the most of it to his wife at the time of his demise. That would be this Virginia Klineschmidt Lake, alias Kohinoor Diamond. The victim."

"Who gets her share now?" The chief perked up. He was always interested in money, like the time the variety store was broken into, he couldn't wait to find out how much they got. Sixty-three dollars and twenty-eight cents. "Wasn't worth it," said Chief Bacon.

"I thought at first it might be one of those deals where it all got divided up among the rest of them. You know, so every one of them could have had a motive. But it seems that the victim, Virginia Klineschmidt Lake, alias Kohinoor

Diamond, went right out and made a new will of her own leaving part and parcel to her sister Annie who was in school at the time."

"And you say this Annie carried on a lot? Could be she was faking that; could be she's your killer."

Vincent tried to keep his face straight. "I don't believe she's it, sir. I just don't believe it. Of course I haven't talked much to her yet. Except for when she was crying and shaking and all, but I didn't learn much from that. Miss Henrietta Lake said she'd just turned twenty. And she doesn't look a bit like a cold-blooded-killer type. Not at all."

"That don't mean nothing." The chief handed Vincent his water cup and Vincent poured it full again.

"I know that. I'm not discounting her. I'm just saying it doesn't look that way to me. Right off the bat, at least. Is it all right if I make that long-distance phone call?"

"To find out about the money business? I guess so, but see if you can get the number and dial it direct because it costs less that way, and you know how Fred Dreer is when it comes to looking over the department bills."

Vincent did, indeed, know, Fred Dreer being the first selectman. Vincent went back to the office and made the call, learned that Annie Klineschmidt was truly what one could call a millionairess and spent the night dreaming that Annie Klineschmidt was in all kinds of trouble, men with daggers coming at her and cars trying to run her over, and all the time, he was the one who kept saving her.

First thing the next morning, Vincent was sitting in the office waiting for a call from Doc Henderson before going out to the Lake place and instead he got a call from Los Angeles, California, of all places, from a newspaper out there; and he'd no sooner hung up before a stranger walked in and said he was from the New York *Times* and what about this Kohinoor Diamond murder and before he could answer, the phone rang again, this time it was a Boston paper; and then there were more visitors from newspapers in New Haven and Hartford and even the area weeklies, and the next thing Detective Vincent Prosper knew, he was being interviewed in front of a television camera.

He told them all the same thing, that Virginia Klineschmidt Lake, alias Kohinoor Diamond (they wrote that down, word for word, he had to tell them how to spell Klineschmidt), had been the victim of a homicide, and the homicide had taken place night before last at the Harrington Lake place where the victim had been surrounded by relatives and a fence with a locked gate and that, so far, that was all he knew.

The New York *Times* man knew about the Lake will, it seemed. "It's a matter of public record when a will's probated." But he didn't sound as though he knew about Annie, not at all, so Vincent didn't tell him. Sensitive young girl like that, it would be awful to have a bunch of noisy, nosey newspapermen on her doorstep; course they couldn't get near the doorstep because of the fence and the gate, but it would be awful just the same right after her sister had been murdered.

When he'd told them all he intended to tell them, which was almost all he knew, he still had trouble getting rid of them. They kept asking questions he couldn't answer, sometimes the same questions over again, just worded differently, and Vincent was getting impatient; he had work to do.

Happily, the phone rang. It was Doc Henderson, reporting in. Vincent used as few words as possible, said, "Uh-huh. Uh-huhhh. Is that so? Well, well. Thanks, Doc." And while he was listening and talking, the reporters were hanging on every word.

When he hung up, he played it like a movie scene. Slowly, he pushed back his chair; it was really the chief's chair; he was in the chief's office. He stood tall and put the tips of his fingers in his pants pockets, thumbs sticking out. Then he said, very slowly, "Gentlemen, I have just received word that Virginia Klineschmidt Lake, alias Kohinoor Diamond, met her demise at approximately 2 A.M. yesterday morning."

"What does that mean?" asked the man from New Haven.

"It means that almost anybody in that house could have done it."

And it did mean just that. Not one of them had an alibi for much after midnight.

XIV

Henny told Annie that there was a policeman to see her, a detective, and so she was surprised to find a young man with very short dark hair, wearing a rather hot-looking suit in a most peculiar tan color, waiting for her in the library. His name, Henny had said, was Detective Prosper, and he'd been there the day before, only Annie didn't remember. She thought he looked just like James Caan except that his hair wasn't curly. She'd seen James Caan on the television; she thought he was handsome.

"I'm real sorry about bothering you, Miss Klineschmidt," the young man said. Annie nodded and looked away. It was almost impossible to believe on this new morning that yesterday they had found her sister floating in the swimming pool. Annie had decided that the thing to do was to pretend it never happened, that Virginia was away, working, and that someday a letter would come from her and perhaps a present.

"I have to ask you a few questions," the young man told her. Henny, sitting beside Annie, patted her hand. "I have to know what time you went to bed the night before last, when you last saw your sister, things like that."

Henny patted her hand again.

Annie thought back. "Last night the doctor gave me something to make me sleep. I slept very well. But the night before"—she glanced at Henny—"Virginia made me go to my room right after dinner. Then she came in and sat with me for a while. She talked to me until I told her she had said all that before."

"What did she talk about?"

"She said the world was our oyster now. I don't know how the world can be an oyster, do you? She said when everybody had gone, she would lock up this house and we would go around the world. She said I must be patient and be a good girl. She said there were people in the world who might like to hurt us in some way, only it wouldn't seem like they'd be hurting us until after it happened. She said did I know about the things men and women do when they're alone? I told her I knew they could make babies, but that I didn't want to make babies. She said she didn't either." Annie studied his face; was that what he wanted to know?

She saw his face redden. He had dark skin, looked as though he'd been in the sun a lot, but even so she could tell that his skin changed colors. She wondered why. "What else did she say?" he asked.

Annie shrugged. "That's about all. She started to tell me all over again and that's when I said I understood and I was tired and wanted to go to sleep. So she waited until I got into my night clothes and then she left."

"About what time?" She thought he looked worried about something now. She wondered what he was worried about.

She caught her lower lip with her upper teeth. "I don't know. I have a wrist watch"—she held up her arm—"but I didn't look at it. I know when I went to bed, though, I looked then. It was about eleven-thirty. After I came up from downstairs."

His expression changed; she thought he wasn't worried any more. "You went downstairs?"

She smiled at him. "I wasn't sleepy. After a little while, I got dressed again and went down. But some of them were

playing bridge and I don't know anything about that game—
it's not like Fish or anything I've played. So I went into the
billiard room and watched Mr. Keltie play that. It's harder
than it looks." She nodded, agreeing with herself. "He let
me try and it's harder than it looks."

"Your sister didn't mention anyone special when she was
talking about people hurting you?"

Annie looked down at her sandals. They were pink to
match many of her dresses. "Adam."

"She thought Adam Lake was trying to hurt you?"

Annie nodded.

"How?"

She looked up at him with guileless eyes. "She didn't tell
me exactly. She just said to stay away from him. I told her
she'd taken care of that. She'd sent them all away. They were
supposed to go. Yesterday." She looked thoughtful. "Now
they can't go, can they? Henny said they had to stay and
talk to the police. That's you, isn't it? You're the police?"

"Yes, ma'am. I mean, miss. The doctor is through with the
autopsy. You can have your sister's body anytime you want."

Annie frowned and Henny said quickly, "We'll arrange for
Mr. Mortimor to handle things." Annie's frown deepened.

Detective Prosper frowned, too, at his notebook, as though
it had disappointed him. "I guess that's all for right now," he
said slowly.

Annie jumped up. "I saw a dog from my window. Is it our
dog, Henny? Can I play with him?"

"Yes, that's Hector. He has a doghouse out in the garden.
You'll probably find him sleeping in the shade somewhere;
he's a very lazy dog except when he sees a rabbit." Henny
smiled up at her. "Why don't you run along?"

Annie beamed, told Prosper, "It was nice meeting you,
detective," and ran out as he struggled to get to his feet.

Henny explained, "She's not exactly retarded, as I understand it. Just immature."

Prosper looked puzzled and distressed. "Immature?"

"I don't mean physically," her tone was dry.

Prosper blushed again, changed the subject. "The victim was knocked unconscious by a blow on the head, a skull fracture, it was. Then she either fell or was pushed into the pool. I've been looking around out there. Have you got any idea what could have been used to knock her unconscious?" He measured with his hands. "Something heavy? Maybe about this big?"

Henny visualized from his gesture an object the size and weight of a round brick. She shook her head.

"I'll just have to keep looking," said Prosper. He referred to another page of his notebook. "I talked to Mr. Benson this morning. He said Miss Annie Klineschmidt was the victim's sole heir, that if the victim had died before her will was made, the money would have gone to charity. He said Mrs. Lake, the victim, made her will with him before she even brought her sister here. He said she was very anxious to settle things, and when I asked him if she acted as though she was afraid something might happen to her, he said he hadn't thought of it that way, but maybe she was."

"I didn't realize that," said Henrietta.

"Usually"—the detective sounded as though he were reciting something he'd memorized—"in these cases, we look for the one who profits most from the death. It would seem that person is Miss Klineschmidt."

Henrietta nodded.

Prosper nodded along with her. "But I just can't see Miss Klineschmidt hitting her sister on the head and pushing her in the pool, somehow I just can't see that."

Henrietta didn't answer.

"Still, I'm not counting it out, you understand. I'm just saying that right now I can't see it."

"Yes, it would be hard to believe."

Prosper nodded once more. "That's why I want to ask you how did Mrs. Lake, the victim, get along with the other people here? Nobody I've talked to so far has said much about that, all too busy telling me how shocked they are and somehow it must have been an accident. But she, the victim, did tell them to leave, didn't she? Sounds like she lost her temper over something. What was it that caused her to ask them to leave?"

"I think she was nervous about Annie. Adam had given her an alcoholic beverage just before dinner, something mild, but it did upset Kohinoor. I mean Mrs. Lake."

"I see. Then that could have been what the victim was talking about when she mentioned people hurting Miss Klineschmidt without seeming to hurt her?"

"I should imagine so."

"Now, how did the victim get along with the other ladies?" He was scribbling in the notebook, looked to be writing in the margin.

"All right. They weren't close friends, I don't mean that. But there was no genuine animosity. We're all different types with different interests and viewpoints. Under those circumstances, there are bound to be disagreements when such people are under the same roof for any length of time."

Another nod. "And, let's see, you were all here, except for Miss Klineschmidt, for over a week, weren't you?"

Henrietta's turn to nod.

"These disagreements you mentioned, what were they about?"

"Oh, minor things. I really can't recall. Things like who

was going to make up a table for bridge, who was going into town with whom. That sort of thing."

"Then you can't give me the name of one of them who might have disliked the victim more than anyone else? I suppose they did dislike the victim? Mr. Benson told me a little how the Harrington Lake will went and I read some in the papers, too. There was bound to be some jealousy, wasn't there?"

Henrietta looked him straight in the eye. "Yes, but nothing serious. My father did remember all of us in his will. None of us need be beggars."

Prosper grunted. He was a very young man to be handling such a weighty problem, Henrietta thought, but he'd explained that Chief Bacon was recuperating from an operation and the town had a very limited police force. He was, she assumed, the best they had. She wondered aloud, "Will you call in the State Police on this? Don't they deal with such serious crimes?"

He looked up. "Oh, I already got in touch with them. They'll come when you ask them. I told them I figured maybe I was doing all right, but I might need some lab help. They said sure thing, to let them know whatever it was I needed, and it was just as well that I was struggling along because they're busy, too."

She asked gently, "You're certain there could be no mistake? I mean, it couldn't have been an accident? It seems to me she could have fallen and hit her head on the pool edge. It seems so much more plausible than—the other."

"Yes, ma'am, I'm certain." He spoke positively, closed his notebook, and stood up. "I'm kind of curious about some of the others, Miss Lake. That Jones fella, for instance. Got any idea where I might find him?"

"Thor or Karl will know. I've been so busy with Annie that I haven't kept track of anyone this morning."

"Okay. I'll just poke around. I'll try not to disturb anybody."

"Thank you, Detective Prosper." She watched him go out the door and listened to him walk down the hall. His father, she thought, ran a gas station on the edge of town. She'd seen the name V. E. Prosper above the pumps. As far as she knew, she'd never laid eyes on the man. Strange, how one could live one's whole life in one place and not know all the people. Probably Thor bought gas for the cars from Prosper's gas station. And here was Prosper's son, grown-up but just barely, a detective.

Henrietta made a move to call Mr. Mortimor about Kohinoor's funeral, but hesitated. She'd have to confer with Annie; Annie certainly had a right to decide how Kohinoor's body was disposed of. But this morning, following a sedated day and a night of drug-induced sleep, Annie acted as though the entire episode had been erased from her mind. Still, Henrietta had to consult her. She went to find her.

And find her she did, sitting happily with Hector in the grassy area next to Henrietta's herb garden. "He's a nice dog," she told Henrietta. "See, he likes me." And she put her face down next to his furry one.

"I have a cat, too, named Dorothy . . ."

Annie lifted her head. "I don't like cats."

"And a parakeet named Bruce."

Annie clapped her hands. "Oh, a bird! I love birds."

Henrietta reached down to her. "Come sit with me over on that bench, Annie. I want to talk to you."

Annie's small frown marred the clear brow, but she obeyed. When they were seated in the shade, Hector followed and flopped at their feet. Annie laughed at that, put her hand

down and rubbed his ears. He laughed back at her, tongue
lolling.

"We must talk about Kohinoor's, I mean, Virginia's, funeral," Henrietta said firmly.

Annie turned her head away. "I don't want to."

"I know you don't, but it must be done. We just can't let
her lie there in that place. We must pay our respects."

Head down, Annie mumbled, "What place? She's just gone
away."

"I understand how you feel, believe me. But if we do this
thing nicely and quickly, then you can forget all about it.
Think, if you will, that she's gone away. Only we must do
this first. Do you see what I mean?"

She peered up through her hair. "You mean . . . bury
her?"

"Yes. Or cremation. Whichever you choose."

"What's cremation?"

"The remains are disposed of by fire. The ashes are left;
it's nice and clean. Like Harry's, my father's, on the mantel."

"Fire?" Annie eyes widened. "She wouldn't like that." She
was silent for a moment, then, "I remember now. She used to
say, 'Bury me in gold lamé!'"

"Yes," said Henrietta, "she did. I heard her."

"Well." Annie stood up. "Then let's do that."

"I don't know . . . I suppose we can find something . . ."
Henrietta was thinking of a theatrical costumer's—where else
could one find a gown of gold lamé? "There's space in the
Lake plot," she went on thinking aloud, "next to Mother and
Audrey; that would be no problem."

"You take care of it all, Henny." And, like a bird darting,
Annie kissed her cheek and was off running, calling to Hector
who reluctantly followed. He was a very lazy dog.

XV

Chief Bacon looked better this afternoon than he had yesterday afternoon, in Vincent's opinion. "I got rid of some of the gas," the chief told him. "They've had me up and walking."

"Glad to hear it. You'll be out of here in no time."

"The doc says I should spend a month at home. How are you doing with the Lake mess?"

"Asking a lot of questions." Vincent pulled out his notebook. "Getting a lot of answers, some of them the truth."

"Roll up my bed a little and let 'er rip. To be honest with you, I need something to think about. I'm beginning to go nutty already. And that daytime television—ugh!"

"Well, I talked to the victim's sister this morning, Miss Annie Klineschmidt."

"Vincent, will you stop reading off their full names every time. I know who you mean."

"She says her sister herded her up to her room right after supper the night she died. Says she told her to watch out for people trying to hurt her. There'd been a blow-up at the dinner table. Miss Lake, Henrietta, says the victim was kissed off at Adam Lake for giving the girl an alcoholic beverage. She, Miss Lake, thinks that the victim was worried about Annie and this Adam and that's why she kicked them all out. They were all due to leave the next morning except Miss Lake, Henrietta."

"Is that the way the others tell it?"

"More or less. Pandora Keltie, now she tries to act like butter wouldn't melt but she can't hide the fact that she had no love at all for the victim. Wanted to know if there was any chance that Annie wasn't the victim's sister but really the victim's kid and that the father came along out of nowhere and killed the victim."

"Well, farfetched and all, but is there any chance?"

"No. In the first place, the victim would have had to be eleven years old when she gave birth, and in the second place, both their birth certificates with the same set of parents are all in order in the Minneapolis courthouse."

"Minneapolis! Another long distance call?"

"Yeah," he said sheepishly.

Bacon sighed. "Fred Dreer is going to have my hide."

"I made another one, too. To a place called Crestwood, New York. That's where Annie was before she came here. It's a special kind of school, very expensive, for kids who have got a screw missing."

"You mean this Annie is some kind of nut?"

"No, not that. They told me a big long name for it, but what it boils down to is this, she got smarter like everybody else until she was ten or so, then she just stopped. But don't take that to mean she's dumb. They told me she was in the upper percentile in the I.Q. department for that kind of thing. It's funny talking to her, sometimes she sounds like a little girl, but she sure doesn't look like one."

Bacon gave him a searching look, so Vincent hurried on to explain that Annie was an heiress who could sleep on a mattress stuffed with hundred-dollar bills if she wanted to, and then he admitted he hadn't been able to find the weapon. "The State lab says it was heavy and smooth, round in shape, and at least a foot long. I poked around but couldn't find anything to fit the bill. I don't know whether it could have been something the killer brought from the house, pre-meditated, or something left around the pool and used on the spur of the moment. She was whacked at the side of the pool terrace, by the way; I found some blood stains. Any-way, when I asked everybody if they had any idea, they all looked blank. I just don't have any ideas—a jug, a vase, they don't figure it was glass or it would have smashed, maybe a hunk of some kind of polished wood? I just don't know."

"You're definitely counting out glass then? Like a bottle or something like that?"

"I think so. If it had busted, they'd have found pieces in her hair. Or on the deck of the pool. It's awful hard to get up every little piece of glass. Course, maybe it didn't break, but the lab boys think that's pretty doubtful."

"Maybe it was metal."

Vincent made a could-be gesture. "Harrington Lake had an Oscar, you know, one of those Academy Awards stat-uettes. I checked it; clean as a whistle like it was polished everyday. I asked the lab boys about that, too. They said it was shaped, would have left marks to indicate its shape. They say this thing, whatever it was, was round and smooth."

"How about a rolling pin?" The chief looked amused.

"A what?"

"A rolling pin. Don't you know what a rolling pin is? Mag-gie and Jiggs?"

"Maggie and Jiggs?"

"Never mind. Before your time. Probably nobody has a rolling pin any more; nobody makes bread and pies, just buy 'em from the supermarket. So, so far you're getting nowhere fast? Except with the telephone bill?"

"Hell, Chief, it's only been a couple of days. Give me time, will you? I don't claim to be any superman."

Chief Bacon closed his eyes. "I'm expecting a visit from

Fred Dreer any day now. He'll want to know why we haven't done something to protect 'the image' of the town. I can just hear him. He's big on this image business." He opened his eyes, grinned. "You looked like a horse's ass on the television news."

Vincent grinned back. "It should have been you. If you weren't boxed up in here . . ."

The chief waved the thought away. "You do better than I would. I'm too old to be in the spotlight. You're welcome to it."

"Maybe Fred Dreer will come to squawk at me instead of you."

"I hope so. I don't wish you no bad luck, but I sincerely hope so."

"Look what that cat is doing," Pandora told Henrietta. "Sharpening his claws in the sofa. He'll ruin it."

"She," Henrietta corrected. "Scat, Dorothy. Go use your scratching post."

"Scratching post! Honestly, I don't know how you can put up with that menagerie." Pandora was putting polish on her fingernails, shell-pink frosted polish carefully applied stroke by stroke. She concentrated on the application as she said, "You've got to speak to that detective person, Henny. If I have to stay here another week with this crew, I'll go mad. Stark, raving mad."

"There really isn't anything I can do about it, Pandora." Henrietta was going over her list for Kohinoor's funeral. The services were to be private, this afternoon, but she was afraid the press people would be outside in force. They'd been plaguing them in person and by phone. Thor kept the big gates locked and no one answered the phone but the staff

who'd learned to say so-and-so is not available for comment
and hang up.

Flowers? Yes, of course, a large family arrangement and a
spray from Annie. Pink roses.

The minister, Pastor Hanson from the Lutheran Church.
It had turned out that Kohinoor was Lutheran.

Henrietta had personally chosen the casket, ordered the
opening of the vault in the family plot. And she'd even managed to come up with a gold lamé dress by means of a telephone call to New York and subsequent delivery by taxi.
Expensive, but then Annie could afford it.

Mr. Mortimor had taken care of everything else. There
would be no calling hours, it just couldn't be arranged with
all those newspaper and TV people about. Telephone calls
of sympathy and telegrams of commiseration would be handled by personal notes. Signed by Annie? She doubted that
she could get the girl to concentrate long enough to write
them, but perhaps she could get her to sign. It would look
odd, two handwritings, but she didn't see how it could be
helped.

"Henny! You aren't listening to me."

"I'm sorry, Pandora. What were you saying?"

"I was saying that Jason and I are anxious to get to the
Riviera for the season. If you aren't in on the beginning, you
miss all the good parties."

"Jason? I thought he was going elsewhere."

Pandora blew on her fingernails. "He's changed his mind.
Or rather, I changed my mind." She looked up at Henrietta.
"Men like Jason are hard to find."

"And costly," said Henrietta mildly.

"I've told him that our life style will have to be modified
to the income. He understands."

Yes, thought Henrietta, I'm sure he does. He understands

that the Riviera is as good a place as any to find a new bene-
factress. Again she felt that pang of pity for Pandora. Who
would be her playmate when she was fifty? Not a cat and a
dog and a parakeet, alas.

"Henrietta?" Pandora pitched her voice very low even
though they were alone.

"Yes?"

"I've been thinking about Kohinoor and who could have
killed her. It seems to me, I know it's a horrible thing to say,
that the only person who really had any reason was Annie.
And she's not all there, of course. If she did do it—wouldn't
that throw out the will that Kohinoor made? Wouldn't the
money revert back to us?"

"You forget about the charities that Mr. Benson mentioned in the earlier proviso. He said if Kohinoor died in-
testate, her share would go to charities. As for Annie being
not all there, I don't believe that's a completely accurate
statement. She is simply somewhat retarded."

"Well, that's the same thing, isn't it? Who's going to manage all that money for her? Some little con man with a be-
guiling smile will have it gone in no time."

Henrietta sighed. "Mr. Benson will help. He's the executor.
I guess someone has to take care of her."

"You?"

Henrietta regarded her soberly. "I don't know who else
it could be." She sighed again. "God knows I don't want the
job. There goes my peace and quiet."

"Then let's get Adam to marry her. That would solve everybody's problem. It would be—all in the family."

"You're asking a great deal of both parties, aren't you?
Besides, she doesn't seem to like Adam very much any more."

Pandora made a face, tested one nail with a tentative finger. "He doesn't exactly grow on you, does he? What's wrong with him, anyway? Something certainly is. Every word he speaks is a sneer."

Henrietta stood up. "I don't know and I don't want to know. Thank heavens, he's not my problem. I think I'll go out in the garden for a little while, Pandora. Don't forget, the funeral's at two, and the limousines will be here at one-thirty."

"I know, you told me. I'll be ready, although I feel like a hypocrite mourning for that woman."

Henrietta did know what was wrong with Adam. Aileen had told her earlier in a tête-à-tête that morning, or, if not told her exactly, had voiced her fears. "Harrington was so wrong when he left Adam such a small amount of money," Aileen had said. "Oh, I know, he thought it would spur him on to greater things, but he doesn't know Adam. How could he? He was so seldom with the boy."

"Twenty thousand dollars isn't exactly peanuts, Aileen. It could give him a start. It's more than many a young man Adam's age has."

Aileen lit a cigarette from the burning butt of the one she'd just smoked. "Do you think I don't know that? I've worked hard, very hard. Sometimes I even enjoy it. But Adam's got—a weak streak. He'd rather win at cards than make the dean's list. In playing cards, he can utilize all his skills—cunning, deviousness—he gets a sense of power." She inhaled, exhaled smoke; her eyes watered. "I'm afraid my son is going to be —no, is a rather nasty young man."

"Aileen!" Henrietta had looked at her with shocked eyes.

"It's true. And that's not all." Nervously, Aileen paced from breakfast table to window and back again. "I'm afraid— I'm terribly afraid he's involved in some sordid affair. He's always after me for money; some of it's gambling debts, I suppose, but then he wins a lot, too. I don't know where it all goes if it isn't to support some little tramp."

"If what you suspect is true, she doesn't necessarily have to be a tramp. Adam seems discerning if nothing else." How glad I am, thought Henrietta, that I never had children.

Aileen shook her head hopelessly. "If only Harrington had given him more. He takes it so personally; it's another rejection. He's very bitter about it. He laughed and told me that he found it very ironic. 'All the Lake holdings in the wee hands of a little moron,' he said. 'From shirtsleeves to chastity belts in one generation, may she rot in hell.' That's what he said and while I'm not sure just what he meant, I'm certain of his feelings. He hates her, he hates his father, and sometimes I think he hates me, too."

"I do hope," mused Henrietta, "that he'll behave at the funeral."

Aileen stared at her. "Behave at the funeral! I'm telling you I'm worried sick about my son and you're afraid he won't behave at the funeral. Good God, Henny, don't you care? He's your brother."

Half-brother, thought Henrietta. "I'm not as callous as I seem, Aileen, but I don't see that there's anything I can do about it. Adam's not a child any more; a good talking to won't straighten anything out. What do you want of me? Just because I'm Harrington Lake's oldest child doesn't make me an oracle. If Adam has problems, the only thing I can suggest is a good psychiatrist. Maybe that twenty thousand would be better spent there than anywhere else."

All the anger drained out of Aileen and she suddenly looked old. "I know," she said, turning away. "Do you think I don't know?"

Detective Prosper, feet on Chief Bacon's desk, held the phone to his ear and listened. With his free hand, he wrote in his notebook. At intervals he said, "Is that so . . . uh-huh . . . yes, I see . . . go on." When the call was finally over and he'd put down the phone, he rubbed his ear gently. The police department's phone bill was going to be pretty high this month, that was for sure. But his notebook pages were filling up. He only wished he could talk to Paris, France, and he would have, too—might as well be hung for a sheep as a goat —but he couldn't speak French worth a damn. Studied it in high school, too, but it was all Greek to him.

He turned pages, began to read, nodding as he did so. Delilah Heap was without an agent these days, but he'd reached her previous agent by telephoning the agency's New York office. The actress had had it, according to the guy he'd talked to. "She never had it, you know? I mean it with a capital *I*, capital *T*. Oh, she was pretty enough in her day, looked like a lady, you know, wore clothes well. But when you get along in years, you've got to have something special in this business. Like Bette Davis, you know? Even she has trouble finding parts now that she's over the halfway mark. But Heap just didn't have it."

Vincent wanted to know about her friends, her social life. The agent said he couldn't tell him anything about today, but, "She never was one of the Rat Pack or any of those cliques, the big-timers. She was kind of dull, you know? Shop talk or clothes talk, that was all. She didn't know how to make little funnies; she wasn't any wit. And not particularly sexy either, if you want my opinion. Maybe when she was real young." He laughed. "Harrington Lake must have married her for something!"

Was she broke? "Probably. No head for business and she's been handling her own dough for several years now."

Did he know anything about her children? "Nah. Never saw them. And she hardly ever mentioned them."

So, for Don and Dawn he'd had to go to another source. Again an agency, a different one, smaller potatoes, specializing more in commercials than epic productions. Another phone call to New York, convince another man that he was an authorized police officer of the law investigating the Lake murder case. The man, his name was Arlen, wasn't happy about speaking to Vincent. "I can't tell you anything except they're pros. If we line them up for anything, they come on time, do their jobs, get their paycheck, that's it." Vincent thought he caught a note of caution in Arlen's tone.

What about their personal lives? The note of caution deepened. "The usual Manhattan bit. Friends in the business. Get-togethers. A little sex now and then, I guess. Don especially. Nothing any cop would be interested in."

"Don drinks quite a lot, doesn't he?"

The answer came clear and strong. "He never lets that interfere with his career."

"Got any idea why he hits the bottle?"

Silence. Then, "Some people do, some people don't. It's a matter of chemistry. At least, that's what they tell me."

"They're twins and twins are something special, that's what they tell me," Vincent retorted. "How do they get along with each other?"

The note of caution returned, stronger than before. "Like brother and sister, what else?"

What else, indeed. Vincent underlined the what else.

The call to Princeton had been to Adam's faculty advisor. Adam's faculty advisor was named Hinton and he had a very cultured voice. "Adam Lake," he said as though they were old buddies, "fine young fellow. Bit of a Peck's Bad Boy at times, but nothing serious. What's he been up to?"

What's a Peck's Bad Boy, Vincent wondered? "I thought probably you'd read about it or seen it on the TV. His stepmother got herself murdered."

"No!" The voice expressed shock. "To tell you the truth, I've just gotten back from an educators' conference in Europe. Do tell me all about it."

Vincent recited the bare facts; Hinton oohed and aahed. His manner changed slightly, seemed he didn't know Adam quite so well, after all. "His social life? Well, I don't know really. I believe he's an avid bridge player, yes, I believe I played with him a time or two. Quite brilliant, perhaps he'll make Grand Master one day, but you don't care about that." He laughed, falsely, Vincent thought. "If only he could apply that brilliance to his studies. His marks are erratic, to say the least. But you probably don't care about that, either. His friends? He doesn't have a roommate this year so that's no help, is it? And last year's roommate dropped out. I wouldn't have the vaguest notion . . . sorry, just thinking out loud. I'm afraid I can't put my finger on any of Adam's intimates. It's my impression, and only an impression, mind you, that he's rather a solitary soul. That doesn't help much, does it?"

No, it didn't help much. But it helped a little because by the time Vincent had hung up, he had the idea that this Hinton was lying in his teeth. Why didn't he want to name any of Adam Lake's friends? The thing to do, if he were a detective in one of those TV cops-and-robbers things, would be to go right down to Princeton; he could just see himself wearing a plaid cap and smoking a pipe, wheeling up in a sports car, bright red that sports car should be. If he were a TV detective, he'd do all that and even grow a mustache. But he wasn't; he couldn't go anywhere, leave town at all because he was needed here. And suppose some other serious crime occurred while he was busy with the Lake case? Heaven forbid, he wasn't twins.

He scratched his nose, looked at his list, dialed information, and got the Washington, D.C. number of the U. S. Passport Agency, Department of State. He dialed direct, as per Bacon's instructions, and that wasn't easy, finally reached a clerk who made him carefully spell the name Pandora Lake Keltie and even Jason Jones. Someone would look into their records and report back to Detective Prosper, she told him. But she couldn't promise anything.

When would they call back? She was equally vague. "What's your name?" asked Vincent in his most official voice. She told him, Mrs. Dunn. Vincent carefully wrote that down with her extension number. "This is very urgent," he told her. "I need information for a murder investigation. Maybe you've heard about it, the victim was the widow of Harrington Lake."

"Oh? Really? Yes, of course, I've been following it closely. Harrington Lake, I just loved him. One of my favorites. I'll see what I can do for you, Detective Prosper. Didn't I see you on television?"

"You might have."

"Yes, yes, I did. I'll see what I can do and call you back as soon as possible."

"Let me call you. I'll be in and out."

"All right. Try this afternoon. I may have something for you then."

Vincent left the Pandora and Jason pages blank, went on to Aileen Lake. At her New York modeling agency, he spoke to her assistant, a Miss Lowe. "I talked to Aileen yesterday; she's so upset," said Miss Lowe. "I don't like to ask for special treatment, but I do hope you'll be kind to her and let her come home as soon as possible. She isn't well, you know."

"She isn't? I didn't know."

"Oh, she doesn't complain. But she's been feeling punk for months now. I think she should have surgery." Her voice dropped. "It's a feminine sort of problem if you know what I mean."

Vincent felt his face flush. Now he didn't know what to ask next. Miss Lowe kept speaking, "I suppose you're looking for some kind of character reference. Well, I can tell you that Aileen is a great gal, one of the greatest. I've been with her for six years and I've never had a better employer. She's fair and honest and a hard worker. And many's the time she's gone out of her way to help a girl in an emergency. Aileen is generous, all heart. But smart, too." Her laugh was self-conscious. "In case you don't get the point, I love the gal."

Vincent got the point and terminated the phone call. The Lakes might be scattered all over the place these days, but they'd lived out at the Lake place in the past, and they'd come into town and maybe the best place to find out anything was in your own back yard.

Vincent wondered who would have the best recollection. Doc Henderson? Sure. Could be. Only he had that patient-doctor privilege thing and he was a kind of a clam most of the time anyway. A minister? The Lakes didn't impress Vincent as being particularly churchy types. Where would they shop? Except for groceries from Martin's, and other necessities, probably New Haven or even New York. But—how about a schoolteacher? All of the Lake sons and daughters had lived here when they had to go to school. And while some of them had gone off to school, could be they started right here. Miss Kinlin, that was the ticket. Miss Kinlin had retired a few years back, but she'd taught first grade for a dog's age. Taught Vincent's mother and father and taught Vincent, too. He looked at the wall clock. If he worked it right, he'd have time to visit Miss Kinlin, grab a hamburg at Ye Olde Dairy Shoppe, and still be in time for the funeral.

Matilda Kinlin had celebrated her seventy-second birthday a few days back and some of her old pupils had given her a little party with a big birthday cake. She had some left over, so she gave Vincent a piece.

She didn't look one day older to him than she had when she taught him nearly twenty years ago. She'd always looked the same, he thought, tall and thin and kind of dried up. Only she wasn't dried up at all; the juices still flowed. Especially the memory juice.

"Of course," she said, pale blue eyes sharp behind her glasses, "I remember them all. Ought to, I had the worst crush on Harrington Lake. From afar, of course. First there was Henrietta, then Pandora, then the twins, and finally little Adam. Only Henrietta went all the way through school here, but they all started with me. And I knew the mothers, too. Not real well, but I knew them. What would you like to know, Vinnie? Will you have another slice of cake?"

"No, thank you, Miss Kinlin. I don't have any special questions; I'm just trying to get an idea of the kind of people they are. I didn't get to know any of them; I must have gone to school between Don and Dawn and Adam, so I didn't run into them. If you could just tell me whatever you recall, it might be a big help."

She gave that some thought. "I'm inclined to say it would be hard for me to believe that any of them committed a capital crime, but that would be a foolish observation, wouldn't it? Still it's hard for me to entertain such thoughts. Now you take Henrietta—quiet, reserved, such a grave little girl. Very intelligent. Very. Her mother was a cunning little woman, like quicksilver. She'd come in a chauffeur-driven car to pick up Henrietta and she'd often come into the school and chat with me for a few minutes. How was Henrietta doing? Was she happy? Did she seem to like the other children, did they like her? Why didn't Henrietta ever invite any of the other children home? I told her I thought Henrietta was one of those youngsters who keep to themselves. I've seen many of them over the years. They're friendly and warmhearted when you get to know them, but they don't really need anyone else. They're quite content to be by themselves."

"Loners, huh?"

"I suppose that term could be used. But it has a connotation of withdrawal that doesn't apply to Henrietta."

"It must have been about that time that her mother killed herself."

"Yes, I remember it well. Such a shock. Both she and Mr. Lake were so well known; that's all anybody talked about for weeks. It was right after Christmas, I believe. I know the child stayed out of school for most of January. I was appalled when I heard about it, absolutely appalled. Why would a woman who had everything, positively everything, take her own life? But I knew that no one has absolutely everything, and I surmised that whatever it was she didn't have, she couldn't live without."

"She slashed her wrists."

Miss Kinlin looked pained. "A terrible thing. How hard it must have been for Henrietta. But when she returned to class, she seemed the same as ever, staunch little thing."

"Did her father bring her to school then?"

"No, he was away, making a picture or doing a play, something, anything to lose himself in his work, I suppose. They had a housekeeper until Harrington Lake married again. Audrey Dell, she was his second wife. Quite a famous singer in her day. Popular music, swing I believe it was. She was a pleasingly plump young woman; she laughed a great deal. Her daughter Pandora was as different from Henrietta as day and night. Pandora was a little beauty and knew it, too. Even in the first grade, the little boys were sitting up and paying attention. She didn't have to depend on brains to make her way."

"Kind of on the dumb side, huh?"

"No, I wouldn't say that. Average. An average intellect. Just not very interested in things scholastic. One can tell at that early age. Frivolous, probably shallow, but eager to please, that was Pandora."

"And her mother drowned."

"Yes, a ghastly thing. The little girl witnessed it. They sent her away to school after that."

"And got another housekeeper?" Vincent licked frosting off his fingers.

"No, I don't believe so. I think Henrietta took over the housekeeping reins after that. She was almost a young woman by that time, quite mature for her age. And then Harrington Lake eventually married Delilah Heap." Miss Kinlin laughed, a high cracked copy of her old chuckle. "That was a big topic of conversation, too. My, did we get a great deal of vicarious excitement from the Lake family."

"So then you taught Don and Dawn."

She nodded. "I used to think of them as the babes in the woods. They came out of that limousine into the schoolhouse, holding hands like little lost waifs. Completely dependent on one another."

"And their mother?"

She pondered. "Not quite at ease in the role of mother-hood. She tried very hard, would appear promptly for teacher's conference; she'd retired temporarily from films at that time. But, it seemed to me, she was always overconcerned about the obvious, or at least about matters I considered obvious. I mean, if she wanted answers to simple child-rearing questions, she could have bought a copy of Dr. Spock."

"What about Adam?"

"A handsome little boy. Looked like an angel." Her tone was dry.

"But he wasn't an angel?"

"Hardly. But I don't hold that against him. I'm suspicious of earthly angels. He just wasn't—a happy child. I can't tell you why. His mother was certainly attentive. Maybe too attentive." She laughed again. "I shouldn't say that. One of the things one learns during a long career is not to make judgments. Are you sure you won't have another slice of cake? I've been keeping it in the refrigerator, but even then, cakes do get stale, you know. And I'd hate to throw any of it out."

"Well, maybe one." He could skip Ye Olde Dairy Shoppe and go right to the funeral. Private, it was, but he'd be there. Sometimes, he figured, you could learn something at a burying.

XVI

Miss Dunn told Vincent confidentially that she'd gone further afield than just the routine passport records. She intimated that she had friends in high places, but her information was, nonetheless, disappointing. Much of which she told him, he already knew. Both Pandora Keltie and Jason Jones spent a good deal of time abroad. Pandora had listed her occupation as tourist; Jason was down as an investment counsel. "I'll bet he's nothing more than an out-and-out gigolo," Miss Dunn sniffed.

"No suspicion of smuggling, drugs, any of that scene?" asked Vincent.

No. But she had a friend in narcotics investigation . . . she'd be happy to check further. Had he found out anything new? She was so interested; Harrington Lake had been wonderful; so sad to think it had come to this.

Vincent told her he was, alas, still in the dark. "I'd appreciate the narcotics check, but I doubt if you'll find anything. Still, you never know. You can get me at this number tomorrow morning."

Well, it might not be as soon as tomorrow, but as soon as she could reach her friend.

"Well, try me here during working hours. If I'm out, I'll get the message." She wanted to talk longer, on his toll charge yet, but he wanted to hang up. He still had to speak to Boston, to Bernard Keltie's boss. And he had to do it today; he had no authority to hold those people any longer unless he wanted to charge them with something, witness necessary to a murder investigation? Did he want to do that? He'd have to go to New Haven and get warrants. Well, if he had to, he had to. But maybe he wouldn't.

Bernard Keltie's boss, named Berger, had a voice like gravel on a tin roof. "Don't talk to me about that s.o.b.," he rasped. "I've fired him. Taking off without a by-your-leave, checks bouncing all over the place; with employees like that, who needs enemies?"

When he stopped sputtering, he told Vincent that Keltie had worked for him for two years, was way over on his draw, seemed always to be in financial difficulties, and had written a check about a week ago to a customer of Berger's that was N.G. "Two hundred clams!" Berger was off again. "I'll have to make it good. What else can I do? If I don't, I lose a customer."

Did Keltie have any other problems like, for instance, woman trouble?

"God forbid! Haven't I got enough? Not that I know of. So far as I know, he kept his nose clean there. If only the jerk had any sense—the sad thing is, he's a hell of a salesman." Berger lowered his voice from a rusty shout. "Tell me the truth, I've talked to him already, when I fired him, he isn't hung up in this murder mess, is he? Because from where I sit, you're all wet if you think he is. Bernie would talk a dog off a meat wagon, but he's no killer. No way!"

Vincent was suddenly tired. "No," he told Berger, "I don't think he's hung up in the Lake killing. Thanks for talking to me, Mr. Berger."

"Hold on—if you talk to the rat, tell him maybe I'll reconsider. If he gets his tail back here and puts in an honest day's work now and again. Tell him, like he knows I got a bad temper. Tell him to call me, will ya? I can't get through to him at that house; they just say he's not available for comment. Comment? What comment? Tell him to call me . . ." and he took a deep breath, added, "collect!"

Vincent told Berger, okay, he would, and hung up. A whole day he'd put in being, he'd hoped, clever. And what had he got for it? Zero.

He'd watched them go into the funeral parlor; he'd slipped in a side door. He'd had a peek at the victim, all laid out in a gold dress, real gold, looking like she'd no doubt looked when living, and that was more than okay. Annie spotted him, peeking in, gave him a startled look and said something to Miss Lake who sat close beside her. Henrietta gave him a quick glance, turned back to listen to the minister. The rest of them, so far as he could tell, sat still and tried not to look bored. But maybe that wasn't a fair statement. He'd gotten the impression that not one of them, except the girl and maybe Henrietta, gave a damn about the victim. And maybe that wasn't so. Somebody certainly gave a damn about her —you don't kill somebody unless you love or hate them.

Anyway, he'd stayed until it was over, that wasn't long. The minister didn't seem to have much to say when it came to the eulogy. Just that she was a loving wife, recently bereaved, a loving sister. Annie started to cry at that point and Henrietta handed her a handkerchief. Then, when it was all over, they slipped out the back way, avoiding, hopefully, the representatives of the news media. But one guy caught onto it and raced down the driveway after the lead limousine.

The TV cameras were grinding as Vincent emerged, and he suffered through another interview, saying, just as he'd said to Miss Dunn, that he was still in the dark. He supposed he should have dressed it up more, but he just couldn't go into that "we are investigating several prime suspects" routine because it wasn't true.

He didn't have any prime suspects. He didn't even have

the murder weapon. And he'd gone so far as to drive out to the Lake place while they were all at the cemetery and ask Ingrid, the cook, if she had a rolling pin.

She glared at him. Of course she had a rolling pin. Any good cook had a rolling pin.

Could he see it? Another glare, rolling pin produced. It wore a flour-covered sleeve; underneath the wood was as clean as a new elm whistle. Just the same, could he borrow the rolling pin? Even as he asked, he looked sadly at the miscellaneous collection of kitchen implements in the drawer it came out of. Did one single member of the household except for the help, and maybe Miss Lake, know where to find it? The help—he wasn't even considering them on his list of —ha, ha—suspects.

"For how long?" Ingrid wanted to know.

"A couple of days."

"How am I going to make noodles?"

"You don't have to make noodles for a couple of days, do you?"

Ingrid looked down at the rolling pin, back at Vincent. "You think maybe somebody used my rolling pin to hit Mrs. Lake?"

"Not really. But I've got to check."

Another glare. "Be sure I get it back clean. You hear? Clean."

Vincent promised, dropped the rolling pin off at the State Police barracks where they'd deliver it to the lab. Rolling pins, for God's sake!

He looked at the wall clock now because he felt tired and it was easier to look at than his watch. He should check in with the chief. Only what did he have to tell him except to expect an even higher phone bill?

As though called upon to pay him back, the phone rang. Vincent picked it up, "Detective Prosper speaking."

"Vinnie, this is Miss Kinlin."

"Yes, Miss Kinlin."

"I've been thinking about our little conversation. I'm afraid I wasn't much help to you, all those old memories."

"You were very helpful, Miss Kinlin."

She ignored the compliment. "I know what you need is up-to-date information. I'm afraid I don't know anyone to call who could tell you anything about most of the people, but there is someone who knows Henrietta, I mean the here-and-now Henrietta, very well. Do you know Ernestine Comstock?"

"Out on Ranch Road?"

"The very one. Ernestine, she prefers to be called Tina but Ernestine is her given name, and Henrietta are bosom gardeners if there is such a thing. I should think a chat with Ernestine might be in order. Henrietta may have told her private things about the family, you see? I can't think of anyone else she might have confided in."

Vincent doubted that Henrietta would have confided private things about the family to anyone, but that was merely his impression of Miss Lake. "Thank you, Miss Kinlin. I'll pay her a visit."

"I still have some cake left, Vinnie."

He realized that she must be very lonely. "I'll try and get by for another piece soon," he promised and hung up, feeling depressed. That was it, he wasn't tired, he was depressed. Because he'd hardly ever felt depressed before, he didn't recognize the feeling. But that's what it was.

Maybe a couple of beers at Mable's Bar and Grill would help. Yes, the more he thought about it . . . There was a tap on the chief's door and Doc Henderson looked in, entered the office.

"Hi, Doc." Vincent swung his feet off the chief's desk. "How are you?"

Henderson didn't answer and Vincent thought, I may be depressed but he looks depressed and tired. He's not getting any younger and he's got a lot of responsibilities, poor old doc.

"You're not busy, are you?" A funny question to ask.

"No. Just going home as a matter of fact. Well, not really home. Over to Mable's." Vincent grinned.

"I don't want to keep you."

"You're not keeping me. I've got plenty of time. Sit down. What can I do for you?"

Doc Henderson didn't seem to hear him. He was staring at a girlie calendar the chief favored. "Something wrong, Doc?" asked Vincent.

The doctor shook his graying head. "I don't think so." He went to a chair, started to sit, hesitated. Is he going to land or isn't he, wondered Vincent? "But that's just the trouble," Henderson said and finally sat down. "I'm not sure."

"Do you want to tell me about it?"

"I'm not sure about that either."

Vincent stared at the doctor and the doctor stared back. Finally Henderson said, "The thing is—with this awful business about the widow, I mean—who would have ever believed such a terrible thing could happen in this town?"

Vincent waited patiently. The only answer to that question was nobody, and the doc knew that.

Doc cleared his throat. "If there was something definite to go on, it would be quite different. You see that, don't you?"

Vincent, seeing nothing, nevertheless nodded.

Henderson's chin sank on his chest; he seemed to be studying his vest buttons. "I didn't think much of it at the time, these things can and do happen. But in the light of recent developments . . ."

Vincent decided to help him out. "Doc, what the hell are you talking about?"

Henderson looked up. Somewhere Vincent had read about eyes that had seen suffering; Doc Henderson's eyes looked like that. "Why, about Harrington Lake, of course. His death."

Vincent, who had been slumping in the chief's swivel chair, slowly straightened up. "What about his death?"

Henderson closed his eyes. "Heart failure. Pure and simple. I'm sure of it."

"Only . . . ?"

"Only . . ." Henderson's eyes snapped open. "He'd had a complete physical just before his marriage. Electrocardiogram and all. His heart was as sound as a dollar." He tried to smile. "As sound as the dollar used to be."

"Well," said Vincent, "if it wasn't heart failure, what could it have been?"

"Oh, it could have been heart failure. A sudden coronary. Blows out the wall of the aorta like an inner tube. It can, and does, happen. It isn't unheard of."

"You didn't do a post-mortem, did you?"

A shake of the gray head, a defensive shake. "He was my patient. He died at home, in bed, at a fairly advanced age. Of seemingly obvious causes. It never entered my mind."

"But now it has."

"In the light of ensuing circumstances."

"You're thinking of poison?"

Henderson sat stiff as a ramrod, whatever a ramrod was, thought Vincent, a rod to ram with, obviously; he told himself he was getting flaky.

"Looking back," the doctor said as though he found it hard to speak, "I don't know."

"But nothing you could recognize right off? Like strychnine or cyanide?"

The head sank again. "Nothing like that. I'm not a fool!" The last sentence wasn't as convincing as the first.

"And Harrington Lake was cremated." Vincent wondered if the lab could tell anything from ashes. Maybe? Who was he kidding? Not poison. Poison doesn't get into the bones.

"Yes," said Henderson glumly.

"So who was at the house when Harrington Lake died?"

It hurt him to speak again. "Henrietta. The widow. The servants, Ingrid and Thor. No, they weren't there that day. It was their day off."

"So what it amounts to is this, we don't know if he was poisoned or not, but he could have been?"

"It is possible. Remote. But possible."

"And if he was poisoned, we don't know by what?"

Doc Henderson nodded unhappily.

"And there were three people in the house plus Ingrid and Thor, only they weren't there because it was their day off?"

"I seem to remember they weren't there."

"Three people in the house including Harrington Lake and his wife, who are now dead?"

Henderson sighed deeply. "That's right."

Vincent stood up. "I want to thank you, Doc. You are a gentleman and a scholar."

"If I'm right"—Dr. Henderson stared at the desk top— "I'm a doddering, incompetent old fool."

"Say not so, Doc. A man of integrity. And even more than that, a man who can face the possibility that he's made a mistake."

"Horse shit," said Dr. Henderson, and his use of that phrase surprised Vincent as much as anything he'd said before.

XVII

Henrietta and Annie watched the TV coverage of the funeral on the six o'clock news. The others were all packing to go home. "Tomorrow," Pandora had vowed. "That foolish young man who calls himself a detective can't keep us here against our will."

"There we are, Henny. In that first car!" Annie pointed excitedly.

The newscasters intoned, "And in one of these somber vehicles there rides, in all probability, a murderer, for these were the people present at the Lake house on the isolated Lake estate when the widow of Harrington Lake was bludgeoned and flung into the swimming pool. There are, if you will, the personae dramatis in this tragedy, along with Detective Vincent Prosper who is in charge of the investigation into the death of the exotic dancer known as Kohinoor Diamond."

"There's that nice detective," Annie cried.

"Detective Prosper"—the TV newsman held a microphone for Vincent—"what's the latest development in this brutal murder?"

Prosper blinked at the camera. "That's not easy to say. Police work is slow, methodical. We are in the process of the initial investigation." He looked pleased with himself and rather surprised at the sound of his words. "I'm afraid there's nothing to report. Yet." He stressed the yet, made it sound ominous.

"Is it true that Kohinoor Diamond was buried in a gown of gold lamé?"

"I don't know just what you call it, but it looked like gold all right."

"We understand that you have not yet identified the murder weapon?"

"I don't care to comment on that at this time. The best way to describe the situation right now is by saying that I'm still in the dark but groping for the light switch." And Prosper grinned, a little foolishly, for the TV audience.

"Is that all?" asked Annie as the newscast went on to other matters.

"It's quite enough," Henrietta told her. She glanced toward the doorway, saw Aileen there. "We've just seen ourselves as others see us."

"Pandora says she's leaving tomorrow. I want to go, too, Henny. Do you think it's all right?"

Henrietta got up, turned off the television. "I really don't know. I think you should ask Detective Prosper."

"I could come back if he needed me, at any time. But I do want to get back to the city. Bernice, Miss Lowe, will need me. She can't run the whole business alone. And Adam must return to school. He has a summer session."

"School," said Annie, wrinkling her nose. "Pfui."

"Bernard is anxious to leave, too. He had an altercation with his employer; he wants to go back and smooth it over." Henrietta looked at her wrist watch. "I wonder if it's too late to call Detective Prosper at the police station. I don't know what hours detectives keep."

"Delilah and the twins are planning to leave if Pandora does." Aileen smiled weakly. "I'm afraid it's no compliment to you, Henny, but the rats are deserting your houseboat."

"It's not my house any more," Henrietta reminded her. "It's Annie's."

"When are we going to have dinner?" asked the owner of the house. "I'm very hungry."

"Around seven-thirty," Henrietta told her. "Why don't you get yourself a root beer? Thor picked some up for you today."

"Oh, goody." She hurried out; the two women watched her go.

"She seems to be taking her sister's death very well," commented Aileen.

"Yes, she seems to be." Henrietta's tone was noncommittal.

"You'd think she'd be terribly distressed. It's bad enough to lose someone dear suddenly, but murder . . ." Aileen reached in the bag she carried, brought forth cigarettes. "I just can't believe it. I don't believe it. There's some kind of mistake."

"I hope you're right."

Aileen lit a cigarette, puffed on it. "And you're very calm. Of course, that's your nature, but doesn't it horrify you? Good heavens, Henny, if this detective is right, one of us killed Kohinoor. That's preposterous!"

Henrietta eyed her. "Adam talked about doing it."

Aileen's thin face paled, then flushed. "You know he didn't mean it; he was only angry. Adam may have his faults, but he's no killer!"

"Who is a killer?" mused Henrietta. "Anyone, they say, will kill if something he loves is threatened. Would you take a life, Aileen, if Adam were threatened?"

"Of course not!"

"Are you sure? I haven't any children, of course, but if someone mutilated Dorothy, for instance, I'd be liable to harm that person back. Kill them? I wouldn't mean to, perhaps, but it could happen."

Aileen looked horrified. "Over an animal? That's horrible."

"So is cruelty," Henrietta spoke gently. "And there are many kinds of cruelty in this world. Sometimes a killing can be an act of mercy."

Aileen looked for and found an ash tray, stubbed out her cigarette. "Don't philosophize about murder to me. Killing is taking a life. That's not to be condoned under any circumstances. I thought you were going to call that detective."

"I'll try," said Henrietta and went to the phone.

She reached him. Aileen could hear his voice from where she stood. Henny asked when they could go home, explained that all were anxious to return to their particular responsibilities.

"Yes, I guess it's all right if they go, Miss Lake. You're going to be there, aren't you? With the girl?"

"Yes, I plan to be here."

"That's good. She needs somebody, you know? Tell her I'm still working on the case; tell her I'm still in the dark but groping for the light switch."

"She heard you say that on television."

"Yeah? I thought it sounded pretty good. Mr. Keltie going back to his job in Boston?"

"Yes, I believe so."

"Fine. Tell them to leave their addresses in case I need to get in touch. And phone numbers, too."

"I shall do that. Thank you, Detective Prosper. The others will be grateful."

And when she'd hung up, Aileen asked, "Then we can go?"

Henrietta nodded.

"Thank God," murmured Aileen. She lit another cigarette.

XVIII

Ernestine Comstock is a crock, that's what the kids used to yell at her when Vincent was a boy. He didn't yell it, well, maybe once, but it wasn't much fun to call people names, he discovered.

Ernestine Comstock was a target because she was fat and had a thick mop of yellow hair that she hardly ever combed, at least it looked that way, and she often had manure on her shoes because she kept a small nursery out on Ranch Road. Not a professional nursery, but she sold plants and shrubs and even trees, and often when someone needed a bush for the bare corner of a lot, they'd go out to Tina's and "see if she's got something."

Vincent found her in her greenhouse the next morning. It was a makeshift greenhouse formed by nailing old sash windows for a shed roof. She was still fat, but not as fat as he remembered, he hadn't seen her for some time, and the yellow hair, now mixed with white, was still uncombed. "Good morning, Miss Comstock," said Vincent politely.

"Mizz Comstock," she said without turning. "M, S, you know. I'm into women's lib." She turned then and looked at him. "You're little Vinnie Prosper, aren't you?"

"Yes, ma'am. I mean, Mizz."

"What can I do for you?" She held up a pot. "Got a nice marguerite here if you're looking for a flower for a girl."

"I'm here on a duty call, Mizz Comstock."

She narrowed her little eyes. "Duty? Now what would that be? Oh, yes, you're a policeman now, aren't you? How's your mother and father? I don't get into town as much as I used to."

"I'm a detective now. They're fine, thank you. I came to ask some questions about gardening."

"Did you now?" She put the pot down. "And since when are detectives interested in gardening?"

"Since I've been working on a case of possible poisoning."

Ernestine wiped her hands on the sides of her smock. Looking at the smock, Vinnie could tell that was a habit. "Poisoning? You don't say? Here? In this town?"

"Well, we're not sure. But in my business, you've got to look into things."

"I can see that. Pull up that stool over there and sit down. Be careful; one leg is wobbly. Who is it you think poisoned who, or can't you tell me?"

"I'm afraid not."

She nodded, he could tell she was thinking over who'd died lately. Some of her front hair fell into her face; she pushed it back and it sort of stood up like a halo. She pulled a second stool out from under a shelf and perched on it. Perched, thought Vincent, wasn't quite the word. She sort of overhung it. "Well," she asked when she was settled, "what can I tell you?"

"What kind of poisons do you use in a garden? I mean, I'd guess there'd be some kind of rodent killer, rabbits can be pretty rough on a row of vegetables, I know."

She was shaking her head. "Not any more. We're off the pesticide kick; you should know that. All these ecologists, they got us doing organic gardening." She laughed. "That means using manure instead of chemical fertilizer. Heck, I always did that."

"Well, maybe some people still use the other stuff. People in the garden club, maybe."

She narrowed her eyes again. "Not that I know of; we're all lambs following the sheep. Any garden club member in particular?"

"Well—Miss Henrietta Lake, for instance."

Thick eyebrows went up, vanished into the low hairline. "Henny? She's the one who started this ecology thing. She knows more about more plants than all the rest of them put together. Maybe even more than me, though I wouldn't want to admit that."

"Still, somebody could have kept some of the old stuff around. What did you use for rodents, anyway?"

"Strychnine. And Henny wouldn't have any around. She's too silly about her pets."

Strychnine. Doc Henderson didn't think it was one of the obvious poisons; he would have recognized it. Vincent was disappointed. "How about DDT? Would that make a human sick?"

Ernestine laughed. "Sure wouldn't make him feel good. But nobody'd down that stuff. It would taste terrible, no matter what you put it in. I'm afraid you're on the wrong track, Vinnie. Whatever track it is."

That depressed feeling was coming back. He supposed there were a dozen things lying around any house that would do somebody in. How was he going to know which when there wasn't any way of checking? He put his feet down from a rung to get off the stool.

"Course you could kill anybody with almost anything that grows in a garden," Ernestine said. "Except for fruits and vegetables, of course."

Vincent put his feet back up on the stool rung. "What do you mean?"

"Well, I mean there are maybe fifty plants that grow around here that are poisonous if you eat 'em. Take the poinsettia. The mistletoe. Laurels, azaleas, rhododendron. Hyacinth bulbs, narcissus, daffodil. Rhubarb leaves. Oleanders. Dieffenbachia . . ."

"Dieffen—what?"

"Dieffenbachia. They call it the dumb cane because if you eat it, you can't talk. It causes an awful burning of the mouth and tongue and you can die from it if the base of the tongue swells enough to block the air passage of the throat."

"Is that so?" Vincent was awed, made a mental note to ask Doc Henderson if Harrington Lake's tongue had swelled.

"Then there's castor beans and rosary pea seeds, foxglove—they use that to make digitalis; larkspur, baneberry, hellebore, pokeweed, lily of the valley, bittersweet, the Christmas rose, the bloodroot . . ."

Vincent took his notebook out, waved her to a stop, asked her to begin again. She repeated the list; he wrote the names down.

"Then there's the underground stems of the iris, the roots of the monkshood, the bulbs of the star-of-Bethlehem, some call that the autumn crocus. The foliage and roots of the bleeding heart, also known as Dutchman's breeches, have been known to kill cattle."

Vincent made a clicking sound with his tongue.

"I'm not through yet. Daphne berries, wisteria seeds and pods, golden-chain seed capsules, they look like beans, you know. The berries of the jessamine, the red sage, Latin name *Lantana camara*, and the yew. Yew foliage, eat some of that and you can go quick without any warning."

"Most of it wouldn't be very appetizing, would it?"

"I'd agree with you, but some people are awful yaps. They'd put anything in their gullet and, of course, some of these things look a lot like eating foods. Now, let's see—what else, right off the top of my head? The leaves and acorn of the oak, almost all parts of the elderberry except the berry, I use that to make wine." She winked. "The black locust, moonseed berries, the water hemlock—that's a bad one, looks like parsley and the roots smell like parsnips. Jack-in-the-pulpit, mayapple, nightshade, the poison hemlock—that resembles a big carrot. Might be easy to add to a stew so long as you didn't forget and eat the stew yourself."

"My God," breathed Vincent, "the woods are one big poison factory."

"Sure thing," Ernestine nodded, hair flew. "Some of these fellas write books about living in the wild, you know. Eat this or that right out of the forest. Now me, I say be mighty wary of eating anything you find growing anywhere. Unless you know it's food, don't nibble."

"Where would I find out more about these things?" Vincent asked. "Symptoms, stuff like that?"

"Heck, that's easy. At the library. They've got books on the subject. Mrs. Morris will find 'em for you. Given you some ideas, have I, Vinnie?"

"You sure have, Mizz Comstock, and I'm very grateful."

"Sure you don't want this pretty marguerite to butter up some pretty young lady?"

"Now that you mention it, Mizz Comstock, I believe I do. How much do I owe you?"

XIX

"Now that everybody's gone, I've given Ingrid and Thor some time off," Henrietta told Annie. "We'll have to do our own cooking tonight."

"Can I help?" Annie was feeding Bruce a bit of apple. He pecked at the piece, said, "Pretty, pretty."

"Yes, if you'd like to. What would you like for dinner?"

"Hamburgers," said Annie, "and maybe hot dogs, too."

Henrietta smiled tolerantly. "I don't believe we have any hot dogs, but we might manage the hamburgers. With a nice salad?"

"Sure." Annie ate a slice of apple herself. "I guess so. I don't like salads very much."

"I make very good ones. With fresh greens right from my own garden."

"It's all right with me." Annie flopped in a chair, stretched. "I probably won't eat much of it."

"Bet you do," said Henrietta. "I'll bet you've never eaten a salad like mine."

Annie shrugged, lost interest. She began to pick at the polish on her fingernails. "It's dull around here with everybody gone."

"I thought you were happy when they left."

"Well, I was. But now it's too quiet. Nobody to talk to. And Hector's too lazy to play."

"You can talk to me."

Annie grunted. "I'd like to go somewhere."

"Where would you like to go?"

"I don't know." She flung her arms up, bent them to hold her head. "To the zoo maybe. I like zoos. Have we got a zoo around here?"

"I'm afraid not." Henrietta had a pile of mending in her lap, slip straps that had come loose, buttons to be tightened, snaps to be resewn. Dorothy wandered into the room, watched the thread move up and down, swished her tail in rhythm. "Why don't you go watch the television?"

"That cat gives me the creeps," Annie stared at Dorothy. Dorothy stared back.

"Cats are very intelligent animals."

"I don't think so. They eat mice. That isn't very smart. Why can't we take a trip somewhere? To Disney World? That would be fun."

Henrietta broke her thread off, folded a slip, put it in the finished pile. "I'm afraid I don't like to travel very much. I'm what you'd call a homebody."

Annie pushed her lower lip out. "Virginia said we'd go round the world."

"Maybe when you get older, you can."

"I don't want to go by myself. I don't know how to get places. I'd be scared."

Henrietta picked up a nylon stocking with a hole in the toe. "Perhaps you'll meet a nice young man and get married. Then he'll take you."

Annie brought her arms down, used her fists to tap methodically at the sides of the chair. "I don't ever want to get married. I don't want to have babies. I don't want to do anything but go to Disney World." Her lower lip came out again. "You've got to take me."

"No," said Henrietta evenly. "I don't want to go to Disney World. Not in the least."

Annie glared at her. "Why? Why don't you?"

"Because I don't want to." Henrietta took small, neat stitches in the stocking toe. "I'm too old, for one thing, and I'm much too comfortable right where I am."

Annie leaned forward. "Please, Henny, please take me. I'll be very good. I promise."

Henrietta shook her head gently, but firmly.

"But why?" Annie's voice rose. "You've got to give me a reason. It's the one thing in the world I want to do, but you won't take me and there's no reason." She whacked the arms of the chair now. "Give me a reason!"

"There is no reason," Henrietta broke the thread again and placed the stocking in the finished pile. Dorothy followed her movements with interested golden eyes. "I'm simply not going. And that's that."

"This is my house," Annie spoke through clamped teeth, "and you've got to do what I say."

"This may be your house"—Henrietta began to sew a blouse button—"but I don't have to do what you say."

"Damn, damn, damn, damn!" When the swearword got no response, Annie darted from the chair, grabbed the folded stocking, and dangled it in front of Dorothy who reached for the nylon with sharp claws, had it full of runners in seconds. Breathing hard, the girl suddenly pulled the stocking away, sending Dorothy rolling with the violence of her quick tug. She held it up for Henrietta to see.

"Very childish," said Henrietta, concentrating on the job at hand.

"I'm not childish!" Annie's eyes were bright; she was close to tears. "You're the one who's being childish!"

Henrietta didn't answer.

"Please, Henny." Wheedling.

Silence.

Annie sat slumped in her chair, hair falling forward over her face. She put her hands together, made a church steeple, looked inside and "saw all the people." She let her hands drop in her lap.

Henrietta sewed. Dorothy got bored and left the room. Bruce ate birdseed and hopped in his cage.

Annie said in a low voice, "You're not ever going to take me anywhere."

"Probably not. Thor can drive you places. That's his job."

"I don't like Thor. He never says anything."

"You probably do enough talking for both of you."

Annie didn't answer.

Then, "I think I'd rather have someone else take care of me. I wish Virginia were here."

"Well, she's not. She's dead and buried."

"She's away—working."

"Have it your own way."

Annie got up, went to the window. "When will you be leaving here? You said you wanted to stay until you got a house of your own."

"This is my house. It may be in your name, but this is my house." Henrietta found this thread hard to break, couldn't reach her scissors, bit through it.

Annie smiled at the window. "But what if I don't want you here? I can make you go." She turned to face Henrietta. "If you won't take me to Disney World, you've got to leave."

Henrietta looked at her thoughtfully. "How will you make me leave?"

"I'll get that lawyer to make you leave. Mr. Benson."

Henrietta smiled. "Mr. Benson is an old friend of the family. And he's arranging for me to be your legal guardian."

"You mean, he'd be on your side?"

"I didn't know we'd taken up sides, but yes, he would."

Annie whirled back to the window. "We'll see," she said softly. "We'll see."

Henrietta made more small neat stitches, this time in the hem of a dress she used for gardening. She'd caught her heel in the hem, pulled part of it down. As she sewed she hummed a little tune. The humming made Annie twitch.

From the hall they heard the sound of the doorbell. "I'll see who it is," cried Annie, running out.

Henrietta stopped sewing, listened to muted voices. The voices grew louder, Annie's and a male's, and they came into the room, Annie and that young detective, Vincent Prosper. He was carrying a potted plant, wrapped in newspaper.

"I brought you ladies a present." He offered the pot to Henrietta.

"Thank you. Put it over there, would you. Why, it's marguerites. Thank you very much. I'll bet you got them from Tina Comstock."

"Yes, ma'am."

"They're one of her specialties this time of year. Won't you sit down?" She put her sewing aside. "Have you any news for us?"

"I'm afraid not." He sat in the chair Annie had occupied. "I just thought I'd come by and see how you ladies were doing."

He looked a little flustered, thought Henrietta. He was watching Annie who, quite aware of his glance, was posing by the bird cage. I do believe, thought Henrietta, he's come a-courting. Froggie's come a-courting, aha, aha. Who said that? Adam?

"You grow a lot of flowers, too, don't you, Miss Lake?" He held his hat awkwardly in his lap. "I like flowers but I don't know much about them."

Well, it was a better topic than the weather, thought Henrietta. "My specialty is dahlias. But they come a little later in the season. Next month."

"They must be pretty." He watched Annie with Bruce. Bruce said, "Pretty, pretty," and Prosper laughed.

"That's all he says," Annie laughed back.

"I'd sure like to see your garden." Prosper looked shyly up at Annie.

"I'm afraid there's nothing much to see now. Just spring things. And they've almost gone by." Henrietta was amused at his clumsy ploy.

"I'll take him through the gardens," Annie offered. "Come on, Detective Prosper, you can meet Hector. He's a nice dog, but lazy."

Prosper looked pleased, stood up. He was carrying something under his hat, that was the reason he'd held it so awkwardly. "Would you? I'm trying to learn. I've got a place in my yard; I thought I'd plant something pretty. My mother likes flowers." He held up the thing he carried. "I've got a book." The book had a plain cover made from a paper bag, like a schoolbook.

"What's the name of the book?" asked Henrietta.

"It tells about wild flowers of New England."

Henrietta smiled. "It's difficult, cultivating wild flowers. Unless you're already blessed with them."

"There may be some. I'm not sure. That's why I wanted to see your garden." He looked at Annie.

Henrietta sighed softly, rose. "Annie doesn't know a lily of the valley from a lady's-slipper. Come along, young man. I'll give you a short course." And as they all went down the garden path, Henrietta leading, she heard him speak softly to the girl, heard Annie's laugh. She was a pretty child; he was no doubt smitten. Better not let him get too interested. With Annie, it was just no use. She'd spend the rest of her life a grown-up child. Very sad, really. But such things happened. If Henrietta had learned anything in her half century, it was that terrible things happened and there was often little one could do but make the best of it.

She pointed out plants, thought how polite he was when he showed interest. Not a very bright young man, but pleasant. He even made notes on a piece of paper inside his book. Perhaps he really was interested; that was curious; it didn't seem to go with his personality. Very few men cared about gardens, especially young men. Why this sudden interest, if it was an interest, on the part of Vincent Prosper? The question intrigued her.

They found Hector asleep under his favorite tree by the small natural pond at the back of the garden. Here Vincent forgot his pretense, because pretense it surely was, and watched Annie play with Hector. Henrietta could see in his face the real purpose of his visit. Should she leave them alone? She had things to do, finish her mending, check food supplies for dinner, ready the greens for salad, take the hamburger from the freezer. "Would you two excuse me? I have some chores to finish."

"Oh." Detective Prosper blushed; how unusual to find a young man who blushed these days. Kohinoor had blushed, too, but Annie didn't. "I'm sorry. I've been taking up your time."

"That's all right. I'll leave Annie to see you out. Unless"— and she eyed him squarely—"there was something else you wanted?"

He blushed again. "No. Thank you very much, Miss Lake."

"My pleasure." She went back down the path, turning once at the bend by the golden chain tree, looking back at them through the yellow-flowered branches. They were sitting on a stone bench, with Hector lying at their feet, deep in conversation. At least, Detective Prosper was deep in conversation. Annie yawned.

"I don't know how to tell you this," Vincent was saying, "and it may not make much sense to you, but be careful what you eat."

Annie stared at him. "But I am careful of what I eat. And I always wash my hands first." Glints of anger sparkled in her eyes. "What do you think I am, stupid or something? I don't go around eating stuff I shouldn't. There was a girl once at Crestwood who ate a caterpillar; it made her sick. It made me sick to think of it. I don't do dumb stuff like that."

"I don't mean dumb stuff like that. I mean, regular food. Like, watch out for things like stews and salads."

"I don't like salads. Virginia used to call it rabbit food. She didn't like salads much either. And"—she wrinkled her pretty brow—"parsnips. She didn't like parsnips. I never ate a parsnip. What do they taste like?"

Vincent thought. "Cinnamon or nutmeg, I'm not sure which; I get them mixed up. They're pale tan in color, shaped kind of like a carrot." He leaned down and scratched Hector's ears. "I wouldn't eat parsnips either if I were you, or carrots."

"Carrots are supposed to be good for you. Either make your hair curly or your eyes bright."

"I know, but sometimes . . ."

"I don't know what you're talking about." Annie crossed her legs at the ankles and swung her feet, bumping Hector who moved but only the necessary number of inches to get out of the way.

He put his hand on her arm. "Listen, this is very important."

She pulled her arm away. "You're trying to scare me and I don't know why." He thought her eyes were like a blue-eyed, terrified animal's. He felt he had gone a little crazy; what was he doing? Sitting here trying to warn a girl, who didn't catch onto things quickly, that her dead sister's step-daughter—God, what a mess, this Lake bunch—might be, just might be, planning to poison her and maybe, just maybe, had poisoned her own father and killed Annie's sister.

It was hopeless. How could he find proof of any of it? And what could he do about this girl who was now prattling on about Disney World? "Want to see my book?" he asked in desperation.

She smiled. Her smile was like sunshine. "I like to read. At Crestwood, I was one of the very best readers."

He handed her the library volume he'd wrapped in brown paper. He hadn't covered a book like that since school days, but he thought Miss Lake shouldn't see the title; she'd be put on her guard.

Annie frowned at the title, read it slowly aloud. "*Poisonous Plants in Your Back Yard.*" She frowned harder. "Now you're trying to scare me again."

"No. I mean, yes. I mean you should be careful; there's a reason. Here, read this." And he found a page, pointed.

"The pretty little girl played house by herself in the landscaped back yard of her parents' home near Cleveland. Her mother heard her hum softly as she set the little table with a tiny cup, plate, and silverware.

"On her plate was a small, bright red radish, a handful of berries, and an apple. With the exaggerated manners of a child playing 'grown-up,' she began her luncheon. Four hours later she passed into a coma.

"Seven hours later, she was dead.

"An autopsy showed that the berries, which she had picked in her mother's rock garden, were a deadly poison. The plant upon which they had grown is known as mezereum, usually called daphne, an old-fashioned garden shrub that flourishes best in rocky places. A native of Europe, this plant is found along roadsides and in gardens from Southern Ontario east to Nova Scotia and south through New England, New York, and some areas of Pennsylvania and Ohio.

"Due to cultivation as a rock garden plant, daphne is also generally scattered throughout the country. There is no known antidote."

She had to ask the meanings of autopsy and coma. She read fairly well, Vincent thought, pronouncing the long words slowly by syllables. "I won't eat anything in the woods," she promised him solemnly. "It's too bad about that little girl. Do we have daphne here?"

"I think so."

"Well, I won't eat any berries then."

"Yes—well, read this, too." And he found a page beyond, read to her, "As a standard rule, never eat anything out of the woods which you believe to be parsley. It is quite possible that it will be one of the most deadly plants known to man —poison hemlock. A native of Europe, it is now common in wet areas in this country. The leaves of this plant are almost identical in size, color, and shape with parsley; the seeds resemble anise or caraway. The roots produce convulsions. Ingestion can cause paralysis which eventually results in death.

"A close cousin to poison hemlock is water hemlock. This plant is almost as poisonous. The danger lies in consuming the roots which resemble dahlia roots and smell like parsnips. Often they are brought to the surface by frost, and a child, finding them and smelling the sweetish odor of parsnips, may be tempted to nibble.

"Symptoms are much the same for both. There is a general weakening of muscular powers, blindness and much bodily pain, although the mind remains clear until death. The stomach of the victim should be immediately emptied."

Annie made a face. "They mean, you should throw up?"

Vincent nodded. "And get a doctor. Right away. And"— spoken so carefully—"even be careful about what you eat in anybody's house. Anybody's. People can make mistakes, you know. Especially when these things are growing all over the place."

Annie nodded dutifully. It was hard to tell what she was thinking as she sat there. There were moments when he felt she understood more than she let on. He tried to see through her eyes, think with her mind. He must seem strange, going on about poisons in a pretty world. And how could he warn her about everything? He couldn't. If that woman wanted to do away with Annie, she could do it. What could stop her with so much ammunition at hand?

He could. How could he have been so dense? He could stop Henrietta Lake by letting her know what he suspected. That ought to insure Annie's life.

He took the book and got to his feet. "I've got to go talk to Miss Lake," he said. "Want to come?"

"No. I'm trying to make Hector take a walk with me. Come on, Hector, get up."

XX

"So I took this book." Vincent held it up for Chief Bacon to look at. "See, it's called *Poisonous Plants in Your Back Yard,* and sure enough, her back yard has got all kinds of them. And I showed it to her. And I as much as told her that if anything happened to Annie, there'd be a thorough police investigation."

The chief looked worried, said, "Whew. What did she say?"

"She just looked at me, nothing seems to rattle that woman, and told me I needn't worry, she was well aware of the 'insidiousness of nature.'"

They were walking, slowly, down the hospital corridor. Chief Bacon's robe was patterned with blue and white polka dots; his slippers went slap-slap. Going to go home, maybe tomorrow, he'd told Vincent.

The chief shook his head. "I'm afraid you've gotten way off track, boy. Just because Doc Henderson's got a doubt in his mind, you jumped to a lot of fancy conclusions. What reason would Miss Lake have for killing her father? And his wife?"

Vincent didn't know, but he could guess at several. "Money? Hatred? Jealousy? Maybe she's just got a screw loose. People like that don't need much reason."

"But you can't prove a thing?"

"Not a thing."

"And nothing about the widow either?"

"I still haven't found the murder weapon." He glanced sideways at the chief. "It wasn't the rolling pin."

"Oh-ho, you looked into that, did you?"

"Sure, I . . . well, you never know."

Chief Bacon, slapping along, looked thoroughly unhappy. "I don't say you haven't done your best. It's your first homicide—me, I've only had half a dozen or so all these years, and they were on the cut-and-dried side. Husband murdered wife or vice versa. Jealous boy friend beat up the 'love of his life.' And then some young punks from New Haven broke into Mable's Bar and Grill one time and shot the night watchman. Nothing that took much brain power on my part, so I can sympathize with you. But just because Doc Henderson has got his doubts, I don't know. He's getting along in years and there's some that say he was never the best doctor that ever came out of medical school."

"Chief Bacon!" A voice called from down the hall. They turned and the chief groaned under his breath. "Fred Dreer," he muttered, then, "How are you, Fred? Nice of you to come see me."

Fred Dreer was tall and bony and walked fast, his angular body seeming to move ahead of his feet. He had what Vincent considered mean, narrow eyes, pearl gray in color and cold-looking. People seemed to take to him, though, for some reason. They kept electing him first selectman.

"You're here, too, Prosper," he said when he reached them. "Good. I want to talk to the pair of you."

"There's a sitting room down here at the end of the hall," the chief told him. "For visitors. Let's go sit; I'm kind of tired."

"If we can talk privately." Dreer's tone was ominous.

Vincent and the chief exchanged glances. Vincent thought maybe Dreer had found out about the telephone calls, but, no, that couldn't be it, the bill hadn't come in yet. The three men walked into the fortunately, or unfortunately, depending on how you looked at it, visiting room, and the chief lowered his bulk gratefully into a chair. "What's up, Fred?" he asked. "You act like you've got a hair across your tail." No coward he, Chief Bacon.

"I've just had a call from Henrietta Lake." Hands on hips, Dreer surveyed Vincent. "She says this one here has been harassing her and her ward."

Vincent wasn't aware that Annie was Miss Lake's ward, but he supposed Miss Lake would fix it so she would be.

"Harassing?" asked the chief. "That's pretty strong language."

Dreer ignored him. "What have you been up to?" he asked Vincent.

"Just talking to them. Politely, but—we are conducting a murder investigation."

"Hah! You got one hell of a way of conducting a murder investigation. I ask questions and I find out that you let the whole bunch go out there, except for Miss Lake and her ward, let them scatter to the ends of the earth. You must be pretty damn sure who the killer is."

Vincent started to say that, well, maybe not damn sure, but he had an idea—the only one that made any sense at all, but he didn't get a chance to say it; the chief started to explain about holding witnesses, but Dreer interrupted.

"Why haven't you arrested him, whoever he is? Why isn't he in jail right now? Hah!" His hahs were irritating, voiced as they were between a shout and a holler. "You don't know who the killer is; got no idea, and you never will. Well, there's one thing I can do and I'm going to do it. Call the state boys in. And don't tell me I haven't got the authority."

"Now, look here, Fred . . ." the chief began.

"Don't look here me. Those newspaper guys, the TV people, they're all going home; they know there's no news here any more. They've got your number, Prosper. Making a fool of yourself on nationwide TV. And a fool of the town, too!"

Vincent then understood one of the things Dreer was so mad about—he, Vincent Prosper, had been interviewed for all the world to see, not First Selectman Fred Dreer. "There's some things about this business you don't know," Vincent told him.

Dreer cut him short. "And there's a lot of things about this business you don't know. I told Miss Lake she didn't have to talk to you any more. For any reason. That you are off the case, as of now." He switched his attention to the chief. "When you get back to your desk, Bacon, we'll talk about this further." And he wheeled on his heel, left them in the after-blast.

The chief called mildly after him, "Thanks for coming to see me, Fred, and cheering me up." He asked Vincent, "What are you going to do?"

"What can I do? Go down to Mable's and have a few beers."

"It's a damned shame." The chief seemed to be talking to himself.

"I know. It would be nice if I could pull a rabbit out of a hat and serve it stewed to Fred Dreer. But any rabbits I can pull out would be half-baked. So I'll go get soused, Chief, and cry in my beer. So long. It's been nice to know you."

"You aren't going to be canned; don't think I'll go for that," Chief Bacon called after him. "Besides, Civil Service wouldn't sit still for it. Not without cause."

"I know." Vincent smiled from the doorway. "I hope I haven't grown out of my uniform." He didn't bother to add that maybe Fred Dreer could find some way of finding cause; he was known to be pretty fair at manipulating things. So what was so hot about being Detective Vincent Prosper? Yeah, what was so hot about that? Yeah.

On the way down in the elevator, Vincent chewed on a thumbnail. He'd had no idea that failure could make a guy feel so bad. But had he failed? How would he know? If nothing happened to Annie, that could mean his message to Miss Lake got across; that wouldn't be failure. Only, if he was all wet and Miss Lake never poisoned anybody, Annie was as safe as houses with or without his help. And Virginia Klineschmidt Lake's murderer would get away with it. Even if it was Miss Lake who was guilty, the way things were now, she'd get away with it. What a mess. It made him feel lousy.

Coming out into the lobby, he nearly bumped into Dr. Henderson, literally. "Hey, Doc," he said, "you got a minute? Can I talk to you?"

The doctor looked beat, even his clothes looked tired. Vincent wondered if he felt all right. He sounded all right. "I was on my way out Fieldtown way, Mrs. Garrett's about to have her eighth; I should slip that woman some birth-control pills, but I guess I've got a minute. Come on, we'll sit in my car."

"Have you done any more thinking on the chance that Harrington Lake was poisoned?" Vincent asked him. He heard the irritation in his voice, realized he was teed-off at Doc Henderson. Knock it off, he told himself. You weren't going anywhere before he stuck his oar in.

"Not much." The doctor sounded truculent. "I did all my thinking before I talked to you."

"And you're still convinced that Miss Lake fed him something to help hurry him along?"

"I'm not convinced, I told you that. I say only that there's a possibility. I've known Henrietta Lake since she was a girl. When she was young, she was what you'd call set in her ways, at least what I'd call set in her ways. Single-minded beneath a meek, good-as-gold exterior. Things had a funny way of happening just the way she wanted them."

"You mean, you think she took things into her own hands

even then?" Vincent couldn't decide whether he'd buy that idea even if it came free.

Dr. Henderson shook his head, took off his glasses, rubbed his eyes. "No. I don't see how. No. But she's lived an unusual life. Harrington was always bringing home new wives, when he came home. It would be only natural for her to resent them and maybe him, especially in her youth." He put his glasses back on. "It's like I told you. I've got nothing to go on, nothing except Harrington's unusually good physical condition. I can't even tell you the symptoms of his fatal illness. Mrs. Lake, his wife, was napping out on the balcony all afternoon, didn't even know he was ailing until it was too late. And I can't tell you what they ate for lunch or breakfast, because it didn't occur to me to look into it, and there was nobody else there but the three of them. You'd have to get that information from the only one left alive, Henrietta, and she could tell you anything she chose to, nobody to prove different." He turned the key he'd left in his ignition. "That's all I can tell you, Vinnie. What you can do with it, I don't know. Me, I've got to go deliver a baby."

Later, into his fourth beer at Mable's, Vinnie told himself it wasn't the title that bothered him so much—he would be the first to admit he was a lousy detective—it was the girl. He was worried about her, real worried. Not for any good reason, for a lot of lousy little reasons. The thought of her bothered him.

He got this shiver down his spine and Mable, who stood six foot four, two hundred eighty pounds, and was named Joe Pelligrino but was called Mable by everybody because that's what the sign out front said and he was too cheap to buy a new sign, gave Vincent a funny look and asked, "What's bugging you, Vinnie?"

"Somebody just walked over my grave, Mable. Give me another Schlitz."

XXI

Annie and Henrietta were in the kitchen. Henrietta was shaping hamburger patties. Annie was slicing onions for the salad and crying a little. "Here, child, take a paper towel. They must be strong onions," Henrietta said.

"I don't like onions," Annie told her.

"They're good for you."

From the front of the house, the doorbell rang. Henrietta looked surprised; Annie said, "Somebody's here. I'll go see who."

"Never mind." Henrietta wiped her hands. "I'll go. It might be one of those newspaper people."

While she was gone, Annie dumped the onions in the salad bowl. She stirred the greens already in it, all kinds of greens, lettuce and spinach and other things she couldn't name. The colors were pretty—tomatoes and pimento-stuffed olives against the shades of green. It was a very nice-looking salad but she wasn't going to eat any of it.

She heard Henny coming down the hall with someone, a man; she could tell from the sound of the footsteps, too heavy for a woman. They weren't speaking and when Henny entered the kitchen first, she looked cross.

"Why, Adam!" Annie was surprised. "I thought you'd gone back to school."

"I forgot my briefcase." Adam smiled his Adam smile for Annie. "It's got my papers and a couple of textbooks in it; I'll need them. Hah, hamburgers and salad. I'm starving. Can I stay for dinner?"

"I didn't see any briefcase up in your room," Henny told him.

"Oh, it must be there. I'm sure I left it. I realized it as soon as we got to the city and I transferred my bags to my own car. But I had to get Mother settled, so I couldn't get away until now." He turned the smile on Henrietta. "Don't worry, sister dear. I'll eat and run. Why don't you be a love and see if it's up there? Look under the bed. That's where I usually leave it."

"Go look yourself," snapped Henrietta. Annie looked at her. Henrietta didn't snap.

Adam shrugged. "Be back in a minute," he told Annie. "I like my burgers rare."

"Now what does he want?" asked Henny when he'd gone.

"He told you. Is there anything else you want me to do?"

"Yes. Set the table, please. For three." Said grudgingly.

"What dishes shall I use?"

"I don't care. The yellow ones. They're good enough."

So Annie was in the dining room when Adam came back downstairs without his briefcase. "I must have left it at school after all," he told her grinning.

She looked at him across the table. "That's kind of dumb, isn't it? Coming all the way back here for no good reason."

"Oh, I had a reason." He pulled out a chair and sat at the table, watching her place salad bowls, silver. "I wanted to see you."

"Why did you want to see me?" Did the fork go on the right or the left? She could never remember.

"I thought maybe we could have a little talk. About money."

"Why should we talk about money? Oh, I see, you want me to give you some. I don't think I'll do that."

"Oh, you might. Because if you don't, I might go down to

see that detective who was always nosing around. What was his name? Oh, yes, Prosper."

"Why should I care if you go talk to any detective?" She went to the sideboard and picked up three yellow plates. She'd like pink dishes. Maybe she'd get some.

"Because I might talk to him about the death of your sister."

She clutched the plates tightly; Henny would be mad if she broke them. "You don't know anything about Virginia. She's away—working."

His grin broadened. His teeth looked very white in the dusk. They heard Henny's footsteps coming from the kitchen and Adam said, "How about a game of pool after dinner? I'll give you odds."

"All right."

"Well," said Henrietta from the doorway, "did you find your papers?"

"Not there. You were right. I left Princeton in such a rush I must have left the case behind. Stupid thing to do. Here, let me take that salad bowl. Uhmmm, looks good." And he reached in, picked out a tomato slice, tasted. "Delicious."

"Yes, it was stupid. Go get the meat platter, would you, Annie? Everything's ready."

"Where's Ingrid and Thor?" Adam was asking when Annie returned.

"They've gone out. You'll have a long drive ahead of you tonight; you'd better leave early."

"Oh, it isn't that far. Don't worry, sister dear. I haven't come back to roost. Give me the rarest hamburger, Annie; that's a good girl. So what's been happening since the exodus? Anything new from the boys in blue?"

"Who are the boys in blue?" Annie wanted to know.

"The police. The cops. The fuzz."

"Detective Prosper doesn't wear blue. He wears regular clothes." Annie scowled at him.

"So he does. You are so literal-minded, little Annie. Give me a heaping bowl of salad, Henny. I could live on it."

"How is Aileen feeling?" Henny asked. "I don't think she looks well."

His eyebrows went up. "Mother? Fit as a fiddle. Just a bit tired from all the excitement."

"She's a nice woman, your mother. I liked her the best of all Harry's wives."

Annie put her fork down with a clang. Henrietta added, "I'm sorry, Annie. I didn't know your sister that well."

"All Father's wives." Adam seemed to wear a perpetual grin tonight; Annie wondered what he found so funny. His eyes were very bright. "It must have been quite an experience for you, Henny, wondering just who he'd bring home next as your new stepmother. And especially this last one, just when you must have relaxed, been thinking he was getting too old."

Henrietta chewed hamburger, then salad.

"Are you jealous of them, Henny?" asked Annie. "Did they make you think of the wicked stepmothers in all the fairy tales?"

"It was Harry's life." Henrietta seemed to have swallowed wrong; she drank from her water glass. "It was my father's life, no business of mine."

"Mother says you were really devoted to the old boy. Did everything for him, when he gave you the chance." Adam took more salad. "Played doggy in his kind-master act."

Henrietta's face was flushed. "He was my father. I loved him."

Adam poised his fork. "You know, something I've always been curious about? Your mother's suicide. How did that happen?"

"You don't mind asking impertinent questions, do you, Adam?" Henny's expression was wooden.

"After all these years? Must be about half a century. Come on, Henny, give me the inside information. Mother says she knows nothing about it."

Henny concentrated on her food. "My mother was a high-strung, nervous person. I was just a child. That's all I know or want to know."

"Oh, come now. You were never stupid, Henny. What was it? Was Audrey Dell already in the wings waiting to come on? Was that what sent her off her rocker?"

"Adam,"—Henrietta looked directly at him—"you are insufferable."

He laughed and they ate in silence.

When they'd finished, Henny said, "Annie, you've hardly eaten a thing. Half a hamburger, and you haven't touched your salad."

"I'm not hungry. I was snacking in the kitchen."

Henrietta sighed. "Well, come help me with the dishes."

"Adam said he'd play pool with me before he left."

"I can wait until you're through with your chores." Adam patted his stomach. "Very filling."

"Go on, then." Henrietta began stacking dishes. "But only one game. We're going to bed early."

"I get the point." Adam grinned. "It won't be long, sister dear, till you're rid of me."

He and Annie walked silently down the hall to the billiards room. He switched on the light above the table, the green felt was so bright it almost hurt the eyes, the corners of the room were in shadow. "You like pool, don't you, Annie? Because you can understand it? Ever played it before you came here?" He turned to shut the door but watched her even as he turned.

"No." She stood staring at the table, seemingly mesmerized.

"You're angry at me," Adam said, selecting a cue. "I know why you're angry. You think I stood you up that first night you came here. When we were going for a moonlight swim."

"I didn't care."

He racked the balls, placed the cue ball in line with them to break the triangular arrangement. "Oh, but I was there. You didn't see me, but I was there."

Annie watched the brightly colored balls fly apart. Adam took aim on the yellow number-one ball, sent it into a pocket with a crash. He straightened up and moved clockwise around the table for the number-two ball.

"Yes," he said as he bent over it, "I lurked in the shrubbery, as it were. I had the idea your sister wasn't too keen on us meeting." The two ball went into a pocket, swish. "And I was right, of course. I saw her sneak down to the pool, hoping to catch us—together."

Annie turned, chose a cue from the rack behind her. Adam was bent over, concentrating on the three ball. Whack, it went flying and he straightened up. "I saw you, too. You'd been playing pool in here with Bernie. You came out looking for me." He smiled. "With the cue in your hand. Bernie must have gone to the john or something. He was drinking beer. No, wait, he'd probably gone to bed. It was late. Well, one way or another——"

"Are you through?" asked Annie.

"Oh, no, I'm still shooting. Where is that four? There it is. I may run the whole table; I feel lucky tonight." He walked around to the other side of the table. "As I was saying, I saw you come out and Kohinoor, your sister, saw you, too. She said why weren't you in bed and you said you weren't a child any more and she said you might as well know the score, you'd never be anything more than a child." He sent the four ball into the far pocket.

"Then you said she lied." He stood straight and chalked his cue. "You said she'd lied because she'd told you that now you could do as you pleased. Then she said you would do as she told you because that was the way it was and always would be." He leaned over for the five ball. "So you whacked her with the cue stick, bam, like a baseball bat and she fell into the pool." The five ball vanished into its hole; he looked up at her. "Then you ran back into the house. I wonder what you wiped the cue stick on?"

"And what did you do?" She was staring, not necessarily at him.

He shrugged. "What could I do? I heard her skull crack when you hit her. If I called for help, I'd have to tell what happened. And that would have gotten you into a whole lot of trouble. They'd have put you in jail and taken all your pretty money away from you. Listen, you should be grateful to me. If I'd told any of the others, they'd have had you behind bars that very night. They resent the fact that you got all the leavings, all the goodies. But I don't, I don't resent you at all, Annie. You're a dear, sweet girl."

She moved back from the table and he laughed. "You think I'm going to make a pass? Fear not, little girl. You're not my type, not at all. To tell you the truth, my type is more on the masculine side, if you know what I mean. No, you probably don't. Well, I did think of wooing and wedding you, although I couldn't have endured bedding you, but after the scene with Kohinoor, I realized I didn't have to go to such lengths. I had only to keep my mouth shut until we could chat. And I did just that. Aren't you pleased?"

Her face was in shadow; he could see only the gleam of her eyes and the sheen of her hair. "Yes, Adam, I'm very pleased."

He looked surprised, but delighted. "Then you'll agree— to give me an income, I mean? I won't be greedy, we'll start off small and see how it goes, maybe fifty thousand at first, see how long that lasts . . ."

She moved forward into the light, carrying her cue. Instinctively he took a step backward, realized what he had done, laughed at himself, then at her. "You wouldn't be so foolish as to wield a cue again, would you? Of course not, they'd get on to you, know for sure this time. Henny would tell them. And besides, the last time you did it in a rage. I imagine if I knew the right questions to ask the right people at that Crestwood school, I'd learn about your rages, Annie. But you don't look angry now, not at all."

"I'm not." She put the cue down on the side of the table. "Maybe you'd better go before Henny gets suspicious. How can I get the money for you?"

"A check would be nice. Good as gold with your signature on it and if anybody asked questions, it would be just because you felt badly about the rooking I got, wanted to help me out. Do you have a checking account?"

She shook her head. "How do I get one?"

"Tell Benson you want one, that's all. It's your money."

"What if he won't give me one?"

"Then you insist. You don't want to be treated like a child, do you?"

"No." She thought a minute. "Maybe I could make Mr. Benson take me to Disney World."

"What?"

"Nothing. I'll call him tomorrow and tell him. I'll send you a check as soon as I can."

"Within a week? I don't think I can wait too long."

"Within a week. You'd better go." She picked up her cue and put it in the rack.

He did the same with his on his side of the room. "You're really a very sensible girl, Annie. People tend to underestimate you." He opened the door for her.

"Do they? What does that mean?"

"It means they don't realize how clever you really are."

"Oh, I've always known that. They think I'm retarded. Some of the kids at Crestwood were—couldn't do the simplest things." She raised her voice, called, "Henny, Adam is going now." There was no answer.

"Don't bother her." Adam yawned. "God, I'm bushed all of a sudden. I'd better get going if I don't want to fall asleep on the road. I've got some no-doze tablets in the car. I'll be hearing from you, Annie. If not"—he grinned—"you'll be hearing from me."

"I know," she said, opening the front door for him. "Good-by, Adam."

She watched him drive slowly away, closed the door, and went into the kitchen. Henrietta was sitting on a stool beside the counter, eyes closed, sponge in hand.

She opened her eyes when Annie entered. "I've had a long day," she said. "I'm tired; almost fell asleep right here."

"I'll finish for you. Adam's gone."

"Good." Henrietta got up, removed her apron. "Just finish putting the dishes in the dishwasher, will you? And the garbage in the disposal. Do you know how to turn them on?"

"Yes, Ingrid showed me when I was in the kitchen the other day. She said if I was going to mess up, I should learn to clean up."

Henrietta patted her shoulder. "You're a good child,

Annie. I'll put the cover on Bruce's cage and take Dorothy up with me. See you in the morning."

"Good night, Henny. Oh—when do Ingrid and Thor get back? Should I leave the door unlocked?"

"No. They have their own key. Besides, they won't be back until sometime tomorrow morning."

"All right. Good night. Pleasant dreams and don't let the bedbugs bite."

Henny turned at the door. "What?"

Annie smiled. "One of the girls at Crestwood used to say that."

"Yes, well, good night."

Annie was awakened by a sound. She turned on her bed-side light, looked at the clock. Just after three A.M. The sound came again; it was a moan; it seemed to come from down the hall, from the direction of Henrietta's room. She got up and slipped on a robe, opened her door, and went down the hall.

She rapped on Henrietta's door, was answered by another moan, a loud one this time. She opened the door and went in. She reached for the light switch; it illuminated a soft light by the bed and another on the bureau. "Are you sick, Henny?" she asked. "Really sick?"

Henrietta's face was the color of her hair. Her eyes were staring, her mouth working. She lay very still as if unable to move. Her mouth finally formed a word. "Doctor."

Annie pulled up a chair and sat down. "Are you in pain, Henny? Where does it hurt?"

"Ag—agony. Hurry."

"It really does work," mused Annie. Henrietta didn't seem to be looking at her, although her eyes were moving. "Can't you see me, Henny? I'm right here."

"Can't—see. Doctor!"

"Oh, I'll call him. But not just yet. There's something I must tell you first. You see, when Detective Prosper was here today—well, yesterday—he gave me the idea that he thought you'd poisoned somebody, Henny. Well, I thought about that and the only person I could think of that you might have poisoned lately was your father. Did you, Henny? Poison your father?"

The mouth moved, tried to move; it seemed to be getting harder for the woman in the bed to form words.

"I guess you can't tell me. I think you could have. After Detective Prosper told me about poison plants in your garden and showed me his book, it had pictures, I looked around and found some poison hemlock, I think it's called. The leaves look like parsley; I put them in the salad when you weren't there, and I found some other plants where the roots smell like parsnips. I remembered that Virginia didn't like parsnips. I think you could have cooked some parsnips and put some of those roots in with them. Maybe you didn't know Virginia didn't like parsnips, maybe you wanted to do away with both of them, I don't know. I guess you got tired of him bringing home new wives all the time and that meant there'd be more babies and the money would be divided more ways and you'd have less and less. Or maybe you were just tired of the whole thing, wanted to be left alone. Are you listening, Henny? Can you hear me?"

The mouth, with great effort, shaped a word; it looked like itch but Annie didn't think that was what it was. Since Henrietta couldn't answer her, she went on, "If you did poison your father, now you know what it felt like. The book said the poison hemlock is one of the most deadly plants known to man. It's very handy to know about such things, very few people do, I should think. And how lucky for me tonight that Adam came. He ate lots of salad, too, if you remember. He's probably on the road somewhere, feeling like you do. Or maybe it hit him before he could stop and ran into something. Serves him right. Adam is really a very horrible man, don't you think?"

With terrible effort, one of the arms of the woman on the bed moved, knocked the lamp over on the bedside table. Annie straightened the lamp, put the phone on the table on the floor. "The book said the mind remains clear," Annie told Henrietta, "so I know you understand me. It will all be over in a little while, I think. I made another little bowl of salad while I was in the kitchen, a new one with no hemlock in it. I also saved some of the other salad. I'll tell Detective Prosper that I didn't eat my salad and I'll give him the good one. I'll tell him that you said one of the others was my bowl, that this was your bowl and that I must have gotten them mixed up when I set the table. He thinks you poisoned your father anyway; he'll think I got the bowl meant for you and you got the bowl meant for me. I'll tell him, too, that Adam came and said you killed Virginia, that's why you poisoned Adam. He'll believe me; I know he will. He likes me."

The eyes of the woman on the bed closed slowly; the breathing was louder. Annie was aware of other eyes watching her, realized that the cat, Dorothy, was staring at her from the window sill. "I'll get rid of you," Annie promised Dorothy. "You know too many things."

Henrietta moaned, a horrible sound. "I'm sorry it's so painful," Annie told her. "I really am. You should have said yes, you'd take me to Disney World."

The corners of Henrietta's mouth came up, almost as though she was laughing. "I'll give you a lovely funeral," Annie said sweetly, "as nice as Virginia's. Would you like to be buried in gold lamé, too?"

XXII

On the Jersey turnpike, the New Jersey State Patrol car slowed as it approached a seemingly abandoned car pulled to the side, half on the shoulder, half on the roadway. The blue light on the top of the patrol car revolved, creating shadowy patterns on the roof of the parked car. A light flashed into the sports car's interior showed the body of a man slumped down in the front seat.

One State trooper opened the door, said, "Hey, you. Wake up." He bent farther in, looked closer, touched the body. He straightened, called to his partner, "Better send for an ambulance. This guy looks bad. I can't get a pulse."

While they waited, they looked into the driver's wallet in the light of the blue dome and flashlight. Adam Lake, age 23, occupation, student. "He sure got a snootful of something," said the first trooper. Asked the other, "What do you think? Booze? Drugs?"

"These days could be anything. Where the hell is that ambulance?"

They heard its siren even before they saw its lights. The vehicle pulled up in back of the patrol car, attendants came from it quickly, brought a stretcher, lifted the body onto it. A tow truck arrived, too, pulled up in back of the ambulance, too close. The driver waved the tow truck back so they could get the body in.

"Is he dead?" asked the second trooper.

"Not yet. I got a pulse, weak, but a pulse." The attendants rolled the stretcher to the ambulance.

"He's sure got a snootful of something," the first trooper told them. "I don't think booze; can't smell it. Something else."

"We'll find out." The attendants picked up the stretcher, slid it into the back of the ambulance.

"Do you think he'll make it?" The second trooper was young, fond of happy endings. It was a nice sports car, a nice-looking kid, no long, dirty hair, no ragged blue jeans, bare feet.

"How the hell should I know?" One attendant reached from inside for the door, to slam it closed. "I'm no doctor." And then the driver took off as an ambulance driver should, siren blaring, screaming in the night.

XXIII

"Vinnie," said Mable, "you're drunk. I told you, you should stick to beer."

"I'm drunk." Vincent had trouble keeping his head off the bar. "I know I am."

"How come, Vinnie? It's not like you."

"Because I blew it. Don't know when—how—but I—blew—it."

"Well—" Mable sighed, and picked up empty glasses off the bar, got ready to close. "Guess we'd better get you home somehow."

Vincent didn't answer. His head was on the bar; he was dead to the world.

"He'll really feel lousy tomorrow," prophesied Mable to Mable. He looked down at Vincent, told him, "You'll wish you were dead."

EPILOGUE

To Whom it May Concern (Whomever finds my body),

In case anything should happen to me before I get around to visiting my lawyer, I am writing this holograph which is, for all intents and purposes, my last will and testament. Please note date, it antecedes other documents.

I, Gordon D. Henderson, doctor of medicine, being an only son of only children and thus, so far as I know, the last of my line, do hereby bequeath all my worldly goods both real and personal to Vincent E. Prosper, Jr., of this town.

So that he will know the reason for my seemingly senseless generosity, suffice it to be said that I owe it to him. He is, to my knowledge, a good but gullible young man who may turn out doing some good in this world if the sharks in the shoals don't get him first.

I'm close to seventy years old as I write this and I'm slowly dying of cancer. For nearly fifty years of my life I've been a doctor, doing my best to heal the sick and live a decent life. But I've failed in many ways and I blame that failure on the fact that I never married, never had anyone to comfort me and keep me. A man isn't born with compassion, at least I wasn't, he learns it from a good woman.

I never married because the only woman I ever wanted to marry couldn't marry me. She was already married and true, that wasn't an insurmountable barrier. She did love me, she told me so, and God knows I loved, still love her. She could have gotten a divorce, her husband was willing, nothing stood in our way or so it seemed. I was young and vigorous, a new doctor, a profession satisfactorily achieved after considerable sacrifice, and I'd found my true mate, what more could I ask?

But the woman I wanted to marry had a child, a daughter. She had been left alone much of her married life to raise this little girl and she was tied to her by deeper bonds than even usual. When she told her daughter that she would soon be divorcing the child's father to remarry, the child was inconsolable, so my love reported to me. She was afraid, she said, that the child would become mentally ill if she separated from the father. I told her this was unlikely, that children often protest loudly such a change in the family structure and that in a short time they generally accepted the new situation. This, I said, would be especially true in this case because the child was so young.

The above was the gist of the last conversation I had with the woman I loved. She went home, promising to try again to reason with the child who did not, by the way, know that I was the man whom her mother would marry, an omission that should have given me pause had I thought seriously about it. In retrospect, it was as though she knew it could never be, and thus, withheld my identity to protect my "good name."

What transpired between my love and this six-year-old, I can only conjecture. The only woman I could ever marry settled her future and mine once and for all. She took her life, she slashed her wrists.

I watched the child grow up. I saw her grow inward, not outward and I thought—this is because she knows she killed her mother. As surely as if she had held the piece of broken drinking glass herself. I know what my love used, you see, because I was called in to examine her body.

I am not mentioning names. Vincent Prosper will know who I mean. The girl, as I say, grew up, grew older. I encountered her often and whenever I did, I think I managed to hide my hatred. Hatred, like the mushroom, grows in dark places. Someday, I vowed, before I died I would see that woman punished.

And at last, I saw my chance. Her father died in her home. I made a deliberately perfunctory examination, termed it coronary occlusion, and signed the death certificate. I waited until a propitious time, how little did I know it would be so propitious, and then planted my carefully cultivated seed of suspicion with Vincent Prosper. I accused her of murdering her father by poison. Would that I could have accused her of murdering her mother.

I need not go on, my heir knows what events ensued. He believed my insinuations, my half-truths, my innuendoes, and he acted accordingly. An older and wiser man would have held back and I would never have lived to see my revenge.

And so I owe a debt to Vincent E. Prosper, Jr. I wonder as I write this whether this legacy will please him, probably not. At least, not at the outset.

But take it, Vinnie, and be grateful. The sharks wait in the shoals and every man needs any handhold in this treacherous sea. I know. They are eating me alive.

Forbes
Bury me in gold lamé